A

Royal

Legacy

Danielle Bourdon

For my mom, Kathy Sleigh
who loved and believed in the Royals
from the beginning

Only the dead have seen the
end of war. --Plato

Chapter One

"Chey, we have a problem. Sander's gone."

"Did you look in the grotto?" Chey, unalarmed at the news her husband couldn't be found, didn't look up from her paperwork.

"Yes. We've looked everywhere."

"The children's rooms?"

"*Everywhere.* He's not on the island, or en route to the mainland, and he's not at the family seat. Security has sent out an alert." The maid fidgeted with her cell phone as if expecting a call any second.

Setting the pen atop the papers, Chey leaned back in her seat. Logs crackled in the large stone fireplace, chasing an unseasonable chill from the room. Her office, a converted chamber in the master suite, provided a place of peace and quiet to do all the work required of a queen. To keep the distractions to a minimum, only a desk, her chair, three bookcases and a chaise lounge decorated the space. No televisions or laptops ever breached the archway entrance.

"Did anyone check the beach?" Chey knew Sander sometimes jogged the shoreline of the island as a way to unwind from the stress and responsibility of being the king of Latvala.

"Yes. Even the other homes close to the castle. His friends. The stables. Someone also went to his father's old hunting cabin in the woods on the mainland. He's gone." The dark haired maid, standing in as Chey's personal assistant while her regular assistant Hanna was out on maternity leave, looked unsure what to do next.

Reaching across the desk for her cell phone, Chey dialed Sander's line. It rang three times and finally went to voicemail. "Sander, call me when you get this. There's a fuss up here because no one can find you." After ending the call, Chey tucked the phone into her pocket and asked, "Have Mattias and Gunnar been notified?" Chey expected so, considering Mattias was first in line to the throne, Gunnar second.

2

"Oh yes. More than an hour ago."

"And this is the first I've heard of it? Why don't you tell me how security knew Sander was missing. For that matter—where is his personal detail?" Chey folded her hands across her lap. After years of marriage to the king, and all they had endured together, Chey knew better than to panic.

Yet.

"He had a meeting—an informal meeting—scheduled for four-thirty this morning. When he didn't show, security began a casual search. It expanded from there. His detail says they never saw him leave the castle. A more through search is underway—the basements, outbuildings, towers."

Places Sander didn't usually go.

Chey glanced at the clock. *6:35 a.m.* She recalled Sander getting up before the crack of dawn, kissing her goodbye, and murmuring something about seeing her later. Beyond that, the details were fuzzy. Sander might conduct crazy morning hours, but she liked to sleep in until five o'clock, at least.

"Thank you, Sarah. Would you ask the sitters to mind the kids?" She rose from her seat.

Sarah inclined her head. "Yes, your hig —Chey."

Chey smiled to put the stand-in assistant at ease. She knew it wasn't easy for the staff to call her and Sander by their first names. Chey couldn't abide all the formality, at least in their home environment, and had put the word out to the employees to go by given names unless they were in the public eye or in the presence of visiting dignitaries.

After Sarah departed, Chey abandoned her office and headed through the master suite. Along the way, she glanced out the tall windows that lined one entire wall. Rising behind a bank of clouds, sunlight streaked toward the sky, creating a fan pattern that turned the very edge of the clouds pink. The photographer in her wanted to snatch up her camera and sit on the balcony for the next hour, capturing picture after picture of the glorious view. She had thousands of similar photos from waiting on the balcony for the sun to rise. The only place better to snap shots was one of the castle towers.

Tightening the belt on her salmon colored, crushed velvet robe (she loved working in her pajamas on early mornings like this), Chey entered Sander's side of the walk in closet and made a beeline for the cubicles holding all his boots and shoes. Surely, she thought to herself, he hadn't done what she was starting to suspect he had done.

If so, she would skin him alive. Slowly.

The bottom row of cubes held Sander's rugged boots, the pairs he wore for riding, working around the castle, and hiking around the cliffs of the island. He had different ones for different tasks, and it was only because she'd known him as long as she had that she recognized exactly which pair was missing. The pair that *shouldn't* be missing at all.

"*Sander Darrion Ahtissari,* I'm going to throttle you to the moon," Chey said. Fishing out her phone, she exited Sander's closet and entered her own.

"Hello?" a masculine voice said before the first ring was done.

"Mattias, it's Chey. Are you on the mainland?" Chey pulled a pair of jeans from a hanger. If anyone could help her do what she needed to do, it was Sander's brother, Mattias.

"Yes. I'm looking for Sander. Did he turn up?"

"Not yet. But I think I know where he

is. Can you have Leander meet me downstairs and arrange a helicopter to fly me to the mainland?" Chey could have arranged the flight herself, but didn't want to waste time arguing with security and advisors about Sander's whereabouts. Mattias could get everything done with no questions asked.

"Where is he?"

"Somewhere."

"That's helpful," Mattias said, a note of amusement replacing his earlier concern.

"He's in an enormous amount of trouble, that's all I'll say." Chey knew better than to spill secrets and sensitive information over these phone lines.

"Trouble of the wife kind? Or trouble of the bodily injury kind?"

"Of the wife kind. I *hope* not the other." She tugged on a pair of favorite, well worn jeans and a long sleeved sweater of white over a thinner shirt beneath. At this late stage of fall, Chey had learned the weather could turn on a dime. One day it might be seventy-two—the next, seventeen. Once, before she'd become accustomed to Latvala's unpredictable winters, she'd been caught on the mainland in a short sleeved shirt when, in the span of three hours, the temperature had dropped and a snowstorm hit. These days, she prepared for the unknown every time she left the castle.

"Why don't you let me come with you," Mattias said.

"Because your security team will want to go and that'll compromise things. If I take Leander, he constitutes enough security for me and no one will ask too many questions." She added socks and knee high boots of black to her attire. Tugging a scarf from a peg on the wall, she wrapped the warm wool around her throat.

"If you even think for a second there could be trouble where ever you're going, then call me back. I'll arrange everything else."

"I will, I promise. Thanks, Mattias." Chey hung up and dialed Sander's number again while she crossed to the door. A distant sound caught her attention, a muted chime-thump-chime. She paused halfway across the suite to listen harder, frowning. Had Sander left a radio on? If so, why hadn't she heard it before now? Following the noise, which abruptly ended as she entered the hall, she quirked her lips and stopped just outside Sander's office.

Pivoting into his sanctuary—this bedroom office allowed him to work in private, the larger, upstairs office used when he had personal meetings with his advisors—she skirted two plush chairs in soft brown leather and drew a bead on the large mahogany desk. Examining his desktop phone, she discovered the alarm function was off. So it hadn't been the alarm bleating music, but something else instead.

On impulse, she dialed Sander's number.

In front of her, muffled by a thick layer of wood, the music came again. This time, she recognized the melody Sander had assigned to her on his cell phone, an upbeat, sexy song from a current and very popular band.

Opening the long rectangular drawer directly in front of his vacant chair, the music blared crystal clear, unimpeded by barriers. The screen on Sander's cell phone read *'Chey',* indicating her incoming call. He'd intentionally left the cell behind, which was both smart and dangerous; anyone might be able to track Sander's whereabouts by GPS and plan a kidnapping. Or worse, an attack. He'd stripped the ability of those people to track him, and at the same time, stripped *her* ability to make contact.

Pocketing his phone as well as her own, she closed the drawer with a little more force than she meant to. A heavy thud echoed through the office.

There was no doubt any longer; she knew where her errant husband had gone. A place he *should* not be, a place that was every bit as dangerous as walking through a minefield for the simple fact that one never knew *precisely* when and where disaster might strike.

Exiting the suite, she paused in the hallway, her mood sinking like the Titanic, and glanced toward her children's bedrooms. It was too early to disturb their sleep. If Elias, her oldest son and the heir to the throne, caught wind of what she was doing, then he would beg and demand and badger her to come along. He was turning out to be as stubborn as his father and as determined as his mother.

Deciding against checking in, which she did religiously every morning, Chey headed to the stairs. In the privacy of her own thoughts, she hoped Sander's brazen foray into the world had gone unnoticed by those who wished him harm.

* * *

Kallaster Castle, with its medieval architecture, stone walls and surrounding ramparts, bustled with activity. Guards stood at attention in strategic locations and others walked the extensive halls, always and ever on alert for trouble. Maids, assistants, castle staff and a plethora of official advisors buzzed through the lower floors like bees, intent on one mission or another. This was every day life at the main seat of the king.

Even after all these years, Chey never tired of the castle's charm. She was as enamored of the high beams arching over the ceiling, the ancient paintings depicting the Ahtissari lineage, and the antiques unique to the castle itself as she'd been the first day she'd arrived. Old flags, armor and weaponry decorated specific walls from different periods of history, giving hints to the country's bloody past. Every now and then she got chills knowing that her children had inherited a legacy that withstood time.

"Excuse me, your Highness," a masculine voice said just as Chey stepped off the last stair.

She knew who that voice belonged to. Urmas, liaison between Sander and his advisors, wouldn't be put off from whatever mission he was on until he got what he wanted. A tall man with salt and pepper hair, distinguished features and a penchant for sternness, he held a file folder in his hands and an expectant look on his face.

"Yes, Mister Urmas?" Chey said. He was one employee that would never think of addressing her by her given name, no matter how many times she asked. Urmas existed in a high state of propriety under any and all circumstances. Chey supposed there was something to be said for consistency.

"Did you have an appointment that I don't know about?" He tilted his head with clear curiosity.

"Yes, I do, and when I leave here, you *still* won't know about it." Chey turned to cross the immense foyer. Her boots echoed off the stone, bouncing around the high domed ceiling.

"Your Highness--"

"Pardon me, Mister Urmas, but I have urgent business." Chey walked through the doors that two guards politely opened and descended the broad set of shallow stairs toward a waiting Hummer. Urmas would just have to wonder where she was going. With Sander's absence causing a stir, she expected Urmas to try and have her followed.

Another guard ushered her into the Hummer's front passenger seat. The door closed on a question from Urmas that Chey pretended not to hear.

Looking across the car, Chey smiled at the driver. "Hello, Leander. Thanks for helping out."

Leander Morgan, brown hair tied half back from the front, dressed in warm clothes in dark colors that allowed him ease of motion, pulled the Hummer away from the steps. He smiled as he said, "Any time. I don't suppose this has anything to do with the missing King, does it?"

It was pointless to deny it. Chey needed Leander's help. Unlike Mattias, who was Sander's brother and heir to the throne should Sander die, Leander had no blood ties to the royal family. He performed dangerous missions with Sander and Mattias and had exemplary skill with weapons, making him the perfect companion for this little mission of her own. "It does. We're going to have to insist that the guards in the vehicle behind us don't get on the helicopter when we get there."

Leander glanced in the rearview mirror as he steered the Hummer toward the towering front gate. The walls that encircled the castle stood high enough that one couldn't see the ocean or the beach on the other side. He said, "There are two cars."

"Two? Urmas is really going all out."

"Care to tell me where we're going?" Leander passed through the gate after a cursory check with the guards. One guard frowned and made a call on his radio, no doubt inquiring why the queen was riding alone with just one guard.

"To the mainland."

Leander laughed. "Well, obviously, since we're taking the helicopter. But *where* after that? And is it the mainland of Latvala?"

"Maybe."

Instead of growing annoyed with her like Urmas might, Leander smiled wider. "There's a reason I like you, your *Highness*. You're just as stubborn as Sander."

"We're three of a kind." Chey, Sander

and Leander. She'd known Leander long enough to know that he didn't do what he didn't want to.

"Exactly. Are we going to lose the guards who will inevitably be waiting on the mainland, too?" he asked, pulling onto a winding road that led away from the castle and the shoreline. A long beach curved away from Kallaster, with trees and other thick foliage taking over where the sand ended. Pallan Island had many rocky outcroppings and minor cliffs, which made the landscape exotic and appealing. At least in Chey's eyes. She'd grown to love this land and its people.

"Yes. I'd feel better if it was just us." Chey watched the landscape while the Hummer picked up speed. The helipad wasn't far. Another two curves and a short straightaway would deliver them to the waiting aircraft.

"Mattias tells me that Sander's detail isn't with him."

"They're not."

"How did he get out without someone seeing him—wait." Leander held up a staying hand. "Sander probably knows more about this island and the castle than anyone, barring his brothers. It shouldn't have been too difficult for him to ditch the guards."

"He's done it before. He even left his phone behind so they couldn't track him via GPS. Speaking of which, we'll have to turn ours off or leave our phones behind once we reach the mainland," Chey said.

"Turning off the GPS doesn't mean they can't locate him if they really want to. They'll just have someone hack it remotely and boom, his cover is blown."

Chey glanced sidelong at Leander. "It never ceases to amaze me that you all know so much about that kind of thing. How to lose security, how to move between countries almost undetected, all of it."

Leander parked the Hummer in a space provided for vehicles near the helipad. He winked. "That's part of our charm."

"It's part of what keeps you all alive, you mean," Chey countered in a wry voice. The men had connections like that because it made their missions easier and less dangerous.

"That, too." Leander climbed out after cutting the engine.

Chey followed. The sound of tires on pavement announced two more vehicles in the parking area. She didn't look over.

"Your Highness," a guard said, trying to get her attention.

Chey paused at the edge of the helipad. "I won't be requiring an escort this time. Leander is all the protection I need for this trip."

"But Your High--"

"I know and understand the protocol. Regardless, I'll be traveling with Mister Morgan for the duration." Chey didn't explain more than that. The longer she dallied, the more chance there was that something could happen to Sander.

Leander held the door to the helicopter open.

Climbing into the back, Chey seated herself and fastened the buckle. Four other guards were talking and gesturing at the edge of the helipad. One was on a radio, probably arranging for security at the main family seat.

Except that's not where they were going.

"Destination, your Highness?" the pilot asked after Leander was seated and strapped in.

"Vogeva. *Do not,* and I repeat, do not announce it over the radio." Chey felt the need to cover their destination as long as possible. Vogeva was a small fishing village up the coast from the Ahtissari family seat on the mainland. Not in another country, but their own.

Leander glanced at her with intent curiosity. His expression was open, inviting her to divulge her secrets.

Chey quirked her lips, letting Leander know she was unhappy about the entire thing without ever saying a word.

The pilot made a gesture of understanding and got the bird airborne.

It wouldn't be long now. Chey covered her ears with the headgear, then twisted her hands in her lap. She inhaled and exhaled several deep breaths to control her nerves. She'd learned the technique over the years of being queen, a way to handle the stress of her position without drawing too much attention to herself.

Leander's hand landed on her arm and squeezed, as if he knew exactly what she was doing and wanted to offer comfort.

Chey smiled a small smile for the gesture. She knew he was also trying to tell her that they would find Sander alive and well.

We better, she thought.

Chapter Two

Vogeva was the quaintest town Chey had ever seen. On previous visits, she'd fallen in love with the coastal village and the clapboard, peak-roofed houses in various colors. Weathered buildings lined the main street, each and every one different from the next. The businesses ranged from a baker to a post office to a boat rental shop. There was a café, a regular restaurant and a clothier. Cobbles had been used for the street itself rather than asphalt, adding to the picturesque appeal. Chey always felt like she was stepping back in time whenever she came here.

After the helicopter landed in a nearby field, Chey trekked across the open landscape toward town with Leander at her side. It wasn't a far walk. The scent of coffee and food wafted on a salty ocean breeze, alluring and enticing.

"Well, this is a surprise," Leander said, as if he was starting to have doubts they would find Sander anywhere near here.

"Not if you know his older habits," Chey said. "To my knowledge, he hasn't done this in a *long* time." Because it wasn't safe to any longer. Chey transitioned from wild grass to cobbles and finally to the wooden plank running the entire length of the front of the businesses.

"It's a sleepy little place, for sure. Is he fishing or something?" Leander asked, keeping an eye out around them.

Chey had faith that Leander could protect them from any unwanted advances or attacks. She knew he had a weapon or two somewhere on his body. Never mind that Leander was quite adept at hand to hand combat. She'd seen it firsthand.

"Probably not fishing, no." Chey couldn't be sure exactly which business Sander might be inhabiting, but she had a good place to start. The café ahead, with its single wood and glass door, served some of the best pastries and coffee in the land. She grabbed the brass handle and entered ahead of Leander, letting her eyes adjust to the dimmer interior. Small tables sat near the front facing windows, while cozy booths lined two walls. A short bar sat straight ahead with round stools for customers. She dragged in a breath, stomach growling at the smells coming from a hidden kitchen.

"Hello, and welcome. What can I get you today?" a waitress asked. She wore sensible clothing—black pants and a simple button down of white—with a full apron over the front. A moment after the waitress asked the question, when she got a good look at Chey's face, she flashed a wide smile. "Last I heard, he'd gone to the docks."

This was what Chey loved about this land and the people. Rather than bow and scrape and call attention to her position by using the honorific, the woman simply acted as if Chey was just another patron. She'd deduced that Chey had come searching for Sander and given up what information she had without hesitation.

Returning the smile with one of her own, Chey inclined her head. "Thank you. I'll check there next."

"Coffee before you go?" the waitress asked, extending the question to Leander by virtue of a glance.

"I'm good for now, thanks," Leander said.

"Maybe on the way out. Thank you again." Chey led Leander out of the café and followed the boardwalk toward the end of the street. Somewhere, between a few of the buildings, she knew narrow alleyways would lead her where she wanted to go. Cutting between two businesses, she took a shortcut to the docks. Clouds had thickened across the early morning sky, blocking out the sun, casting a gray pall over the landscape.

A few fishermen nodded respectfully in passing as she and Leander emerged on the backside of the businesses. Docks ran the length of the waterfront here, set apart from the stores by a broad, cobbled street used for deliveries and to offload supplies from incoming boats. There were more people here, mostly men, bundled in thick sweatshirts or jackets, beanie type hats and gloves to combat the chill. A group down the way seemed to be readying to go out fishing, and another pair of men were rolling up a long net.

Her gaze landed on a docked boat and four men who offloaded sacks of grain or rice or some other non-perishable food. The distinct size of one of the men was a dead giveaway. Taller, broader and more muscular than his companions, the man wore an old pair of yellow slickers and heavy weather boots. The long sleeved white thermal hugged his broad back and followed the contours of his big arms. Blonde strands of hair inched out from beneath a navy skullcap, further assuring Chey she had the right man. Veering that direction, she led the way toward the quartet, her boots thudding on the docks. She shot Leander a quelling look when he rumbled a quiet laugh, having also spied the errant king doing common chores.

Leander cleared his throat but could not *quite* subdue all his humor.

As a sack landed atop the growing pile, Chey marched up behind Sander with the intent of tapping him sweetly on the shoulder to announce her presence. Instead, before her finger could poke his body, she suddenly found herself wrapped in a strong pair of arms and twisted around until she was helplessly trapped against Sander's chest, staring up at his scowling face.

"How did you know it was--" Her question got cut off by a question (or two) of Sander's own.

"What are you doing here? Where are your guards?"

Chey returned Sander's glare. He

looked scruffy, his whiskers covering the better part of his jaw. "I could say the same thing about *you,* your Majesty. I don't see any security in sight at all." After a moment, she added, "And you smell like fish."

One of the other men unloading sacks of grain laughed. Otherwise, the men continued to offload, unaffected that the king and queen of Latvala were having a mild marital spat. Leander stepped past, clapped Sander amicably on the shoulder, and began hauling sacks to the docks in his place.

"You shouldn't worry about my welfare. I can take care of myself," Sander said with a stern frown.

"So can I."

"Really."

"Yes, really. Haven't I proven it time and again?"

"You've proven to be a real handful, that's what you've proven."

Chey almost ruined it and smiled. He never failed to catch her off guard when they were bantering or 'arguing'. She had a hard time resisting him when he got stern like this, and the longer she stared into his bluer than blue eyes, the more she melted inside. "You're one to talk," she scoffed, drawing a ragged laugh out of him.

"Is that so?"

"Yes, that's so."

"And what do you think you're going to do about it? Hm? I've got the upper hand here," he pointed out.

Chey could think of far worse positions to be in than trapped against Sander's chest, his arms securing her body to his. "You've put yourself in a bad position, is what you've done, because all I have to do is perform a sideways ninja move and you'll wind up in the bay."

"Crushed between boats, too. I'll be a cardboard cutout of a man in your bed after that, and how fun would that be?"

Chey imagined Sander compressed into a cardboard cutout and laughed out loud. He took advantage and kissed her. Chey wrapped one hand around the back of his neck, lingering in the affection until Leander pointedly cleared his throat.

"I thought Sander was In Big Trouble," Leander said. One could almost hear the capitals on the appropriate words.

Chey broke away from the kiss, amused at Leander's retort. "He is. Just because he got a kiss doesn't mean he isn't grounded."

Three sailors and Leander all laughed at the same time. Sander snorted and tilted Chey into a straighter, upright position. He did not let her go. "You don't have the authority to ground me, Missus Ahtissari. I do what I want, when I want."

"We'll see how arrogant and haughty you are when I suddenly have a headache for two weeks in a row."

Sander looked taken aback. "You wouldn't dare."

Chey let her brows float upwards as if to say, *wouldn't I?* In reality, she'd be hurting herself as much as she'd be hurting him. Chey enjoyed his affection as much as he enjoyed hers.

In the background, Leander muttered, "You're in it now, brother."

A devilish grin cut across Sander's mouth when he heard Leander, but he never took his eyes off Chey. In a slightly raspy, sexy voice, he said, "I bet I could change your mind."

Chey wasn't about to deny it. Not when he looked at her like that, and sounded like he wanted to nibble all her most sensitive places. She shuddered, then batted his shoulder. "Let me go. You don't play fair at all."

Laughing a boisterous laugh, Sander

kissed her once more then released her. "We're almost done here, then we can go."

Chey stood aside as Sander rejoined the efforts to finish unloading the grain. Secretly, she loved how personable he was with his countrymen, how he didn't mind getting his hands dirty to do 'real work'. She remembered how he used to visit the small villages along Latvala's coastline before he was king, stopping to talk or have coffee with the natives. He'd won many citizen's loyalty over that, people who supported him still. Those days were supposed to be over, the days of taking leisurely strolls in the open, alone. Sander's advisors and Generals would have a fit if they knew he'd been here all along, working alongside the fishermen, unprotected from attack.

If she was honest with herself, *she* wasn't that happy either, not after he'd nearly died when his own brother had blown up a convoy he'd been riding in. Those had been frightening days Chey would never forget.

Losing Sander scared her more than anything.

Admiring the flex of muscle while he worked, Chey considered ways to make sure this didn't happen again. At the same time, she cringed inwardly at the thought of taking something he treasured away. This was a release for him, kept him intimately connected with his people. He *enjoyed* being among them, getting to know them, being one of them. She also didn't want to see him dead. He was entirely unprotected out here from a sniper, which he couldn't fend off from fifty yards away. One of the fishermen could be an undercover spy and dump him over the boat before anyone knew what happened. They weren't, and for that she was thankful.

Once the last sack hit the dock, Sander clasped hands with the men and bade them goodbye. Leander did the same. Circling his arm around her hips, Sander escorted Chey down the docks to the walkway.

"So, where to now? Don't suppose we have time to stop for breakfast before we make the trip back to Pallan Island?" he asked with a boyish grin.

"Sander--"

"I know, I know. That puts us *both* out in the open and at risk. I feel safe enough to eat with Leander at our side. What say you, brother? Up for a meal?" Sander slanted a look askance to Leander.

"I'm starving. Let's do it." Leander clapped his hands together in anticipation.

Chey couldn't argue with their boisterous good mood. "If anything happens to you, Sander Darrion, I'll hurt you. Real bad."

"That sounds enjoyable. You should up the stakes of your threats, love," he retorted.

She laughed and batted him in the stomach. "Just take us to eat already."

"Whatever you say."

Chey couldn't help but keep a worried eye on the calm streets of the city as they made their way to Sander's favorite restaurant. The men might not be outwardly worried, but she worried enough for all three of them.

She'd learned by bitter experience that no one could predict when or where an attack might occur.

* * *

Seated next to Sander in a cozy booth, Chey forked up the last bite of her hash and potatoes. Covered with cooked egg, the meal was a favorite though one she didn't eat often. Used to a lighter type of

28

breakfast, Chey nevertheless enjoyed the rich fare while the men devoured every single thing on their plates. Sander had a hearty appetite anyway, what with his constant training and exercise. Today was no different.

The fishermen and other dock workers that came and went from the mountain-themed restaurant all paid their respects to their king in the same casual manner as the rest. Chey was able to relax at least a little and appreciate the smooth polish on the natural wood table, the weathered walls and the large potbelly stove that took up a large portion of the middle of the room. When customers were chilled, all they had to do was add wood from a covered stack just behind the stove.

As the waitress poured another round of coffee, Leander cupped his hands around his mug and asked, "So, how are things in the hinterlands? Making progress?"

"Better than they were last year, and the year before that." Sander grunted and quirked his lips.

"But still struggling?" Leander asked.

"A little. What's been surprising is how some people bought so deeply into

Paavo's lies. They still think he might get free and come to implement the false changes he promised." Sander turned his mug a half circle but didn't lift it for a sip.

Chey watched Sander aside, understanding a lot more about his reaction to Leander's question than he let on. Years ago, his brother Paavo had attempted a coup. Sander had wound up in the hospital and Chey had been accosted and taken to a distant castle in the kingdom. Paavo had nearly succeeded in his quest to become king. Many innocent people had perished during the mayhem, with Paavo pitting certain citizens against one another; those loyal to him, and those loyal to Sander. Regaining control of his country, Sander worked hard to mend the broken ties with the people. Things were not optimal, yet he had made incredible strides as far as Chey was concerned. He was only one man, and his tireless determination to get Latvala back on solid footing was slowly coming to fruition. Leander had a huge hand in helping right the wrongs, though he hadn't been to the hinterlands in some time.

"Speaking of Paavo—what *are* you going to do with him? Continue to leave him in the traitor's prison? I hear he doesn't suffer," Leander said.

Sander scrubbed his fingers through his whiskers. "That's where he belongs. Some of the citizens don't agree with it. They think we should give him another try. But they weren't there to see the men dying of burn wounds and worse when Paavo ordered the strike on my convoy. Good soldiers were lost. Wives and children lost husbands and fathers. That was the lesser of his atrocities, so no, I won't be letting Paavo out of prison any time soon."

"I agree with you. He forfeited his chance at redemption with the taking of so many lives." Leander, matter-of-fact about Paavo's circumstance, had another drink of his coffee. "I'd heard a few bureaucrats recently demanded the issue be brought to the attention of the council and feared there might be a vote."

"They can squawk all they want to. Paavo will remain behind bars." Sander sipped the hot coffee.

"Sometimes, it seems the bureaucrats aren't really for Latvala's interests at all. It makes me wonder where their true allegiance lies," Chey added. This was a hot topic between her and Sander of late.

Several of the lobbyists had been demanding more trade between Latvala and other countries, or easier access to Latvala's assets. Chey added, "Often, I get the impression they want to sell off portions of the country to the highest bidder."

Sander shot her a disgruntled but agreeable look. "It matters what I say in the end, and I'll die before allowing foreign interests to permanently take control of any of our land."

"I hope so. I mean—not that I want you dead," Leander hastened to say, grinning at the awkward way the wording came out. He grew serious a moment later. "But that you don't sell pieces of the country off for money. I can name countless other countries who have done the same and are now in deep trouble."

"It won't happen here. You can be sure of it." Sander set his mug down after another swallow and palmed the warm earthenware. His hands were so big they dwarfed the vessel.

"I'm glad to know you're sticking to your guns. Mattias was just grumbling the other day about the very same things. He is also not predisposed to giving the lobbyists what they want," Leander said.

Sander smiled knowingly. "My brother and I are of the same mind about our country. Gunnar as well."

Chey reached a hand down to lay it atop Sander's thigh, a casual sort of intimacy in the otherwise serious discussion. Gunnar, Sander's youngest brother, was following in his and Mattias's footsteps. He was a prince worthy of the title.

"Thank God," Leander retorted. "I'd have to find new kings and princes to offer my services to."

Chey laughed at the same time as Sander. Leander was a trusted friend and confidant to them both. As well as the husband of Chey's best friend, Wynn. Chey couldn't imagine life without Leander and Wynn in it.

"If anyone would have you," Sander added.

"It's the steep price I charge. Few princes can afford me." Leander puffed his chest up, then exhaled a laugh.

Chey scoffed while Sander snorted. Chey said, "You no doubt have to charge exorbitant prices to appease Wynn's shopping sprees."

Leander slapped a hand over his heart melodramatically. "Don't mention the shopping sprees, you cruel woman."

Amused, Chey sipped the coffee then set down her cup. "I do try and curtail her spending habits when we go out."

Sander barked a laugh and reached down to squeeze Chey's hand. "That is the biggest line of bull I've ever heard. Now let's go before you try and tell Leander that your sprees are for the good of the country or some nonsense."

"It *is* good for the country! Wynn and I heartily support the talented tailors and shop owners in the cities."

The men rolled their eyes in playful exaggeration and slid from the booth. Sander laid down a hefty tip for the waitress. Hand in hand, Chey allowed Sander to lead her to the exit. Leander stepped out first, on alert for anything unusual or suspicious. He signaled the all clear.

Disaster, at least for today, had been averted.

Arriving at the waiting helicopter fifteen minutes later, the pilot twisted in the seat to deliver a message to Sander once they'd embarked. "Your Highness, you're needed at the main castle. It's urgent."

Maybe disaster hadn't been averted

after all.

Chapter Three

On the flight to the Ahtissari family seat, Sander contemplated what urgent matter had arisen this time. It had been years since anything of a serious nature—such as the coup that almost de-throned him—occurred within the borders of Latvala. He wouldn't have described the prior years as peaceful, exactly, but there had been no more overthrow attempts, no political catastrophes, no uprisings in the back country where his brother had sown the most seeds of discontent among the citizens. The economy was prosperous and every day, more and more people showed solidarity to the king. It took time to recover from the despair that had gripped his country in the aftermath of Paavo's attacks.

Perhaps it was nothing more 'urgent' than the lobbyists once again demanding attention. Or the advisors wanting approval to propose documents to the council about additional import and export deals.

Everyone wanted *something* from the king.

Disembarking with Chey and Leander at his side, Sander strode to the waiting limousine and handed his wife into the car before sliding in himself. Leander came last after surveying the flat land around the helipad.

The short ride to the castle passed in silence. Sander's mind was on business and he wasn't wont to conjecture about what might await him in the conference room.

He eyed the immense castle, surrounded by high walls, with mixed emotions. The main family seat was not his favorite place to be. Whenever possible, he held all his meetings at Kallaster castle on Pallan Island, the castle he had inherited upon ascending the throne. He preferred its more medieval flare and the inherent privacy the island afforded him. Kallaster had its share of advisors, lawyers and diplomats, but nothing compared to the family seat.

He didn't notice any extra security at the looming iron gate that rumbled up at their arrival, a good sign in his estimation. If a threat had come in, there would have been another layer of men outside the castle walls and more in the turrets standing at each corner. Sander exchanged a knowing glance with Leander; the man was smart enough to be taking notice of the same things and filing away the information for later.

Inside the walls, the limousine followed a concrete drive toward the broad front steps. Guards in military dress stood at attention as he disembarked. Sander turned back to Chey and said, "How about I meet up with you upstairs when we're done?" He needed a quick shower and a change of clothing before he could show his face in the conference room.

Chey had been right. He *did* smell like fish.

"I'll be in the informal parlor," she said, standing on her tiptoes to kiss his mouth.

Sander resisted the temptation to hook an arm around her waist and haul her to him. He *could* offer to take her to the king's suite, but he knew she would prove too much of a distraction. "Excellent. I'll text you now that I have my phone back." Chey had returned it on the ride back from Vogeva.

"Hurry up."

"I'll text you when I'm good and ready,

wench," he retorted, using an old term of endearment. Corralling Chey in the crook of his arm, he escorted her up the stairs with Leander at his other side.

Passing through the open doors, Sander parted from Chey, then paused to address Leander in a low voice that wouldn't carry. "Wait around until I know what's going on, in case I need you?"

Leander inclined his head. "I planned on it. I'll nose around the staff and see if anyone is talking."

"I'll be in touch as soon as I can." He clapped Leander on the shoulder, then turned to cross the foyer for the steps. As opposed to the stone and wood theme of Kallaster, the Ahtissari stronghold was a collection of marble floors, painted walls and gilt trimmings. It still had excellent defense mechanisms such as the surrounding ramparts, the iron gate and turrets with guards who kept an eye out for enemies. The interior, with extensive crown molding and baroque architecture, was a world more refined than Kallaster. This stronghold was the prime destination for visiting dignitaries and foreign guests. There were entire wings dedicated to harboring ambassadors or sovereign rulers and all their staff.

Rising to the 'family' floor, the level that housed royalty and the king and queen, Sander bypassed more guards and entered the king's suite after navigating numerous hallways. This current King's suite wasn't the same one his father had occupied during his reign. Sander had attempted to live there once or twice, though an entire redesign and remodel hadn't been able to remove the odd pall that hung over the chamber, as if Aksel were watching from some otherworldly domain. Sander ordered another room in the hall remade into something he and Chey could live in for the short durations they were at the family seat. This chamber wasn't quite as large or luxurious, but it was spacious enough for a living area, his and hers bathrooms, two large closets, two offices and a bedroom with a double king sized bed.

After a shower, he spared a moment to shave the scruff off his jaw. Scraping his fingers back through his damp, shoulder length hair, he let it dry on its own while he sought a clean pair of black slacks, a grayish-silver button down, matching black suit jacket and contrasting tie. By the time he was done, polished shoes and cologne in place, he looked ready to tackle the advisors and councilmen.

Departing the suite, he strode with purpose along the hallways to the stairs. Descending at a quick clip, he met Urmas, who had come over from Pallan Island, in the foyer.

"Which room?" he asked his liaison.

"The King's conference room, your Majesty." Urmas fell into step at Sander's side. "An important matter has been presented by King Konstantine of Imatra."

Sander snapped a look sideways at his assistant. "What important matter is that?"

"The advisors are being close-mouthed until your arrival. There is quite an uproar, however."

Sander refrained from more questions. Urmas wasn't in the know, unusual in its own right, and it was pointless to hammer him for answers he didn't have. Taking a separate hallway, Sander made his way to the King's conference room, a chamber set apart from the other meeting and conference rooms. He couldn't imagine what Konstantine wanted. The neighboring king of Imatra—a country separated from Latvala only by another, smaller country—was a man of intensity and ambition. Konstantine had come into reign the year prior after the sudden death of his father and had thrown Imatra into turmoil when he'd fired more than half his father's staff to bring in his own men. Whispers surfaced through the lower ranking employees that in the latter few months, Konstantine had suffered the threat of his country falling under the control of Russia, who had advanced armies—so it was said—all the way to Imatra's border. Sander had sent several spies to the back country of Latvala to make sure the same wasn't happening in his own proverbial backyard. Not only had there been no sign of the Russians, more information had come through other sources that insisted Konstantine had fabricated the story to gain sympathy from world powers who had then sent him money and weaponry in case he found himself fighting for his throne. Konstantine had built a questionable reputation during his reign thus far, forcing other world leaders to warily watch from the sidelines.

Men rose to their feet when Sander entered the chamber. He inclined his head in greeting and acknowledgement before taking a seat at a head table facing the rows of chairs occupied by advisors and councilmen.

"Your Majesty, we will get right to the point," Hektor, the speaker said. "Konstantine sent word directly that a skirmish has taken place on the border between Imatra and Russia. Eight Imatra soldiers were killed when Russians advanced on a small village in Imatra's territory. Konstantine's ambassador assured us during his visit that the situation is dire. Communication was intercepted that leads Imatra's Generals to believe the Russians are planning another, larger strike."

Crossing the chamber, Hektor set several photographs on the king's desk. Color pictures of death and destruction.

Sander slid one photo aside to view the next. He recognized a charred Russian flag amongst the bloody bodies sprawled across the ground. What struck him immediately was the coincidence of a Russian flag being anywhere near what surely had been an unannounced advance across the border. Why would Russia blatantly carry a full sized flag into a skirmish?

"And what does Konstantine want from Latvala?" Sander asked, perusing a few more pictures. One or two were quite gruesome. Slain men in unnatural poses, eyes staring into whatever heaven or hell awaited.

"Your Majesty..." Hektor paused, licked his lips.

Sander glanced up. It was the sudden, subtle change in Hektor's voice and demeanor that snagged his attention. Not only urgency, but an electric excitement that Hektor seemed barely able to contain. Sander waited Hektor out.

"...Konstantine has proposed a most interesting solution. He wants Imatra and Latvala to join forces."

Sander would never understand why some men all but salivated at the idea of war. Battle was not exciting or frivolous or something to be looked forward to. It was bloody and dangerous and frightening. It was true that Sander enjoyed the smaller missions he sometimes accompanied a few of his acquaintances on, but he and his brethren were always trying to *save* people, not kill them.

"I'm not sending troops to Imatra. As far as I know, the Russians are not knocking on our back door, and I will not send our men and women in to fight a skirmish that Imatra is able to handle."

Sander scooted the photos into a pile and scanned the rows of council and advisors in the opposite chairs, sussing out the general feel of the crowd. Some men seemed appalled at the idea, and others looked in support of the proposition.

"Your Majesty--"

"The answer is no. Konstantine's army is more than capable of chasing back a few Russians."

"But--"

"Do you have any proof that the Russians are advancing on Latvala?" Sander asked the crowd at large.

Men shifted in their chairs and looked generally uncomfortable.

"That's what I thought," Sander said, standing from his seat. "My answer is no."

From the back row, a council member stood as well. He said, "You are quick to send more Imatra men to their deaths--"

"Would you rather it be *your* sons or daughters?" Sander said, holding tightly to his temper. "Hm? Paulus? Aigar? How about your six sons between you? Should we send them to fight the Russians?" He met each man's eyes as he strolled from his desk to the rows of ascending chairs. Sander wanted to drive his point home, *all* the way home. "How easy it is for you men in your expensive suits and pampered lives to throw soldiers into battle at your whim. A battle we're not positive exists. One infraction does not a war make."

Paulus and Aigar cleared their throats and looked down at the papers in their hands. Several other advisors refused to meet Sander's eyes.

"I agree with you, your Majesty. We should not get involved," someone in the back row, a supporter of Sander's policy, said.

"What, and allow the Russians to invade our neighbor to the north? If the Russians take Imatra, there is only Somero standing between us and the Russians. I don't need to tell you that the country of Somero is half the size of Latvala and would be easy to invade," someone else retorted. "Konstantine believes Imatra is only the first. Somero and Latvala could be next."

"Where is your proof? A few pictures does not make a truth. Yes, there are dead men in those pictures and yes, there is a Russian flag suspiciously placed under an Imatra soldier. When was the last time a country invaded on foot, supposedly wishing an element of surprise, toting a very large flag to announce their presence? The medieval age? I challenge the stupidity of that action. The Russians are not that dumb, gentlemen." Sander stalked back and forth before the rows of chairs, meeting the gaze of whoever was brave enough to look his way. Some men did in obvious agreement of his deduction, and others either studied papers in their hands or eyed him as if they wished someone with more bloodlust was king.

"We have Konstantine's word," one man dared to say. "Why would he lie? What does he stand to gain?"

"If he was that concerned about an all out invasion of his country, he would have come to talk to me himself," Sander countered. A rush of whispers swept through the members.

"He does wish an audience with you," Hektor added.

"Then why isn't he here?"

"His ambassador said that if you were hesitant to send aid--"

"Oh, I see. I'm only good enough to meet with in person if he doesn't get his way." Sander clenched his jaw, teeth grinding in annoyance. "I am not convinced this situation is as threatening as the king would have us believe. For now we stand down." And that was that. Sander didn't stick around to hear more arguments. He departed the chamber while the advisors and councilmen broke into fresh discussion—if it could be called that. He left them to it.

Right then, there were only three people he wanted to talk to, and none of them had the title of councilman or advisor attached to his name.

* * *

On his way up the stairs, Sander pulled out his phone and shot Chey a text.

Meet me in the informal parlor when you're ready. He jogged up the final steps and cut down the first hallway on the royal floor. This level, reserved for the immediate family and a select few others, was much quieter than the rest of the castle. His brothers Mattias and Gunnar chose to live in their personal castles elsewhere in Latvala, only staying at the family seat when duty demanded it. Like Sander, his brothers had few good memories in this place. Natalia, his only sister, was off with her Balkan prince in another part of the world.

Entering the informal parlor, Sander expected to have to wait for Chey. Just as he started to send off a text to Mattias, he spotted his wife in one of the wingback chairs, staring into the distance out the windows. Although 'informal', the room still had a wealth of crown molding, a tall fireplace and a few gilt trimmed pieces of furniture interspersed with sofas and chairs that provided more comfort than the rest.

Striding quietly up behind Chey, Sander leaned around the corner of the chair and brushed a kiss against her temple. She twitched in surprise, proving she hadn't heard him coming.

"Oh, hi. I didn't know you were here." Chey smiled when she glanced up.

Tempted to, Sander kissed her again, this time on the mouth. "Didn't you get my text?"

"I don't know." She pulled her phone from the pocket of her jeans. "It's here. I just didn't hear the chime. How did the meeting go?"

He sat in the chair across from her, lounging back with his legs sprawled before him. "Not good."

"What happened?" She frowned, cupping the cell phone in her hand.

Sander shot off a few more texts. Mattias, Gunnar, Leander. He needed a meeting as soon as he was done with Chey. Looking up, he said, "The king of Imatra, that's the country next to Somero which borders Latvala, wants me to send troops to fight what he's calling a skirmish with the Russians."

Chey's frown deepened. "What's going on with the Russians?"

"I don't know. I *do* know that they're not pushing against the back border of Latvala. I've had men doing periodic checks ever since the whispers began that there was unrest in the other country."

"Are you sending troops to Imatra? What does he mean by 'skirmish', exactly?" Chey asked.

He studied Chey's face, framed by layers of loose dark hair. She was still as beautiful in his eyes as the day he'd met her. The spark of curiosity in her blue eyes vied with concern for Latvala's soldiers, countrymen she had claimed as her own.

"No, I'm not. I wasn't convinced things are as bad as Konstantine wants me to believe. Never mind he didn't even bother to come talk to me himself. I told the council that if he really thought the Russians were going to invade, he would have been on my doorstep immediately. It's not wise to rush troops off at the drop of a hat. A strong show of support with Imatra—whom we do no trade with, nor are allies with—could possibly put us in Russia's crosshairs *if* they are lining up at Imatra's borders. Until I have more proof that there's a problem, our troops stay here."

"I take it the councilmen didn't like it?"

"Some believe as I do that we shouldn't rush to judgment. There was mention of 'joining up' with Imatra, though I'm not sure exactly what that means. Of course there are others who feel as if we're allowing a further invasion if we *don't* get involved. There is never one hundred percent agreement on anything." Sander always expected there to be division among the advisors and councilmen.

"Do you think they'll drop it now? Leave it alone?"

"It's hard to say. Konstantine wants a meeting with me. Not before asking for aid, but *after* I'd said no." Sander didn't want to rush to judgment on Konstantine, either, considering he didn't know the king well at all. Although 'neighbors', Latvala and Imatra had never had close ties. It still rankled that the king hadn't bothered to come himself if the situation was that serious. Sander meant to force his hand; if Konstanine and Imatra *were* being invaded, he figured he would see more proof from other sources. That changed the game considerably, but didn't mean he would automatically send his men into battle.

"Are you going to do it? Have a meeting?" Chey asked with a curious lilt to her voice.

"I'll probably have to, just to cover my backside. If I disregard the meeting and it comes out later that he was desperate for help and I ignored him, it wouldn't look good for Latvala. I don't want to give off the wrong impression for the country. We've had enough bad press to last a century."

"Soon, then?"

"In the next day or two, I imagine. I'm going to have a talk shortly with Mattias, Gunnar and Leander and fill them in, but I wanted to drop by here first to let you know what's going on." He stood up out of the chair.

"You know I always appreciate when

you keep me clued in, especially with matters like this. I'll see you later this evening, all right?" Chey rose from her chair, too, and met him halfway.

He encouraged the wrap of her arms around his middle while he engulfed her in his embrace. "You'll definitely see me later. I love you."

"I love you, too," she said in a quiet voice.

Sander kissed her one more time before stepping around her for the door.

Chapter Four

"So you think he may be exaggerating the threat?" Gunnar Ahtissari asked.

Sander let his gaze drift from his youngest brother to Mattias, then to Leander, and finally out the windows to the flatlands surrounding the back half of Ahtissari castle. The open area had been cleared of trees centuries ago to allow better visibility of approaching armies. Acres and acres of pastureland stood between the castle and the start of the forest. The coastline, with its stunning view of jagged rocks and the incessant lap of the ocean, stood exactly opposite of the forest. Sander couldn't see the water from this angle, but occasionally heard the horn of a passing boat.

"I don't know. Something doesn't sit right with me, though. That Russian flag tangled up with the bodies looked..." Sander sought the right word. "...*planted* there. It seemed out of place with the rest of the picture. I can't put my finger on it, but the entire scene appeared staged. I've seen battle zones, been right in the middle of them, and they were nothing like what I saw."

"What would be Konstantine's reasoning, then, to stage such a thing?" Mattias asked. He ran a hand back through the short, styled layers of his dark hair. Mattias's equally dark eyes remained on Sander.

"I'm baffled by it. I don't have a good guess," Sander admitted. "He wants troops from Latvala—but to fight what enemy? That 'conflict' was just a skirmish and he lost men. Konstantine's army had to have driven the Russians back across the border, or the meeting of kings would have been much more urgent than it was. There should be a news blast on every world station and so far, nothing about an invasion, even a minor infraction, has made the media. Combined together, it's coming up strange in my book."

"I agree. We should not send troops until we know more," Gunnar said. Blonde like Sander, the youngest Ahtissari brother crossed his arms over his chest. Leaner than the king, Gunnar was still broad through the shoulders with honed muscles from long sessions of training.

"Go with your gut instinct. If something felt off about the photo, then that's probably the case," Mattias added.

"And you said he wants to meet with you if your answer was no. That's interesting. I can't wait to hear what he has to say," Leander said.

"Me as well." Sander glanced at Leander, then looked back to the distant treeline. "I'll tell you one thing, though. I'm not going into that meeting blind. I think it's time for another, more thorough border check."

"How many are going?" Leander said.

Sander might have laughed at Leander's quick reply and obvious eagerness, except this was no laughing matter. "I think the three of us should do."

"Wait, three?" Gunnar frowned.

Sander stepped aside to clap his younger brother on the shoulder. An amiable gesture to appease the affront he was about to deliver. Gunnar had been training hard for missions of this kind, yet Sander needed a trusted pair of eyes in the castle while he sought more answers. "Yes. You need to stay here and take charge while we're gone."

"But Sander--"

"I know, I know. How will you get more real time experience unless you're active in these forays. I understand that, but this time, I need you here, brother. God forbid anything happens, we need an Ahtissari to take the throne." With Sander and Mattias going together, that left only Gunnar as an eligible heir in the event of a catastrophe. Sander's son, Elias, wasn't old enough to ascend. Wouldn't be for a very long time. Gunnar would provide a workable, stand-in king until Elias was of age. Sander wouldn't risk the throne falling into the hands of whatever other sovereign cared to invade should all three brothers die. Paavo, their other brother, was currently serving a life sentence by Sander's command.

"All right." Gunnar inclined his head, accepting his lot with grace.

Sander had seen his youngest sibling mature by leaps and strides these last years. Gunnar was turning into a fine, capable prince and warrior in his own right. He squeezed Gunnar's shoulder then turned to Mattias and Leander.

"Ready for a trip to the hinterlands, boys?"

* * *

"I still don't understand why you can't send someone else," Chey said. She walked a slow path from an overstuffed chair to the cold fireplace and back again. Having returned to the informal parlor at Sander's request, she'd listened to his plan with Leander and Mattias and couldn't help but try once more to get Sander to send men in his stead.

"I *can*. I can send anyone. But they might miss something important that Leander, Mattias or I won't. I want to see for myself if the Russians are testing the borders that back our countries," Sander said.

"But you just did that, didn't you? Not long ago?"

"Yes. A cursory check by men who were not on serious alert. And that was before. This is now, *after* a supposed incursion that happened recently. Likely, we'll find nothing more than scrub and brush and a few dead trees." Sander braced his hands on the back of a chair.

Chey felt his gaze track her every step. She hated the pangs of fear that kept trying to surface at the idea of Sander that far out in the hinterlands without easy access to medical attention. The hinterlands, a desolate area spanning thousands of acres at the furthest eastern border, had few amenities and no hospitals. Only the bravest natives had homes there and those were spread far and wide. A person could walk for days and days without seeing a single sign of humanity. If there *were* skirmishes going on, and *if* the Russians were beginning a press into smaller coastal countries, then, in her opinion, Sander was leaving himself wide open for attack. Yet they had been through variations of this before, when he chose to put himself in the path of danger for the benefit of his country or the safety of someone else. She'd promised to be more understanding, to work with him when these situations arose—and she *had.* She'd been very good about the secretive missions he sometimes went on, putting his own life in immediate peril.

"I know you worry," Sander added, before she could say something else. "But we're careful, and we know what we're doing. This particular visit will be like looking for a needle in a haystack, as it were, and will probably amount to us wandering the hinterlands without seeing anything worth while. Which is good, all told."

Chey circled the chair, wandering closer, as if drawn to her husband by some magnetic pull. Sander had always had that effect on her. He straightened as she drew within arms reach and palmed her hip to draw her the rest of the way into his body. Chey rested a hand on his chest and stared into his eyes. She enjoyed seeing him all dressed up like this and though she liked scrubbing her fingers through his whiskers, she had a thing about his clean shaven jaw. The smooth skin felt good against her cheek when she rubbed against his like a cat.

"Just call me when you get back. How long will you be gone?" Chey capitulated, not wanting to argue or have tension between them right before parting ways.

Sander pulled her snug against his chest. "Two days, maybe three. Not that long."

Long enough, Chey thought. "All right. Be careful."

"You know we will. Return to Pallan Island, though, rather than bringing the kids here. I don't want them at the Ahtissari stronghold any more than need be," he said, bending to press a lingering kiss against her lips.

Chey caught him around the nape and held him there for another minute more. She tugged his lower lip with her teeth and flirted a little with her eyes. "I know. I'll go home as soon as you depart. I don't want to be here, either." Chey and Sander felt equally troubled in the family seat and never stayed longer than was necessary.

"Good. Give the kids hugs and kisses from Daddy and tell them I'll be back soon, hm?" He dipped his head to nuzzle at her throat.

"If you keep this up, your little adventure will be delayed for hours and hours," Chey said with a small noise of contentment for the nip of his teeth at her pulse.

"You're a wicked distraction. And if you think I won't make my brother and Leander wait a little longer, you're absolutely wrong."

"Really? Is that a promise?" Chey gasped when Sander suddenly picked her up while she was still pressed against him. He walked with her through the room to the nearest wall, trapping her between it and his body. Catching the edge of her shirt, he dragged it up her torso. "Less talk, more touching."

* * *

Chey stared at the water as the helicopter flew her back to Pallan Island. The slate gray surface reflected the deepening color of the sky, which had turned dark and brooding during the stolen hour Chey spent with Sander in the parlor. Her body still tingled from the rough handling and a delicious ache had settled low in her pelvis from the animalistic pounding of Sander's hips. A stray shiver coursed down her spine at the erotic memories of their coupling. He'd left her all but starry eyed in the aftermath, spent of passion and more in love than ever.

She smiled to herself as the first glimpse of Pallan's shores came into view out the window. What a lucky woman she was to have found a man like Sander. Compassionate, intense, attentive, thoughtful, and one hell of a lover. One hell of a king, too. She couldn't imagine anyone else fulfilling the role Sander had in her life. Although she had struggled with some aspects of becoming queen, she'd learned to suppress most of the stress and strain, finding other outlets like exercise or photography to help unburden her mind. There had been a lot of growth on her part, she knew, since her coronation. Being Sander's wife came with complicated responsibilities that challenged her, forcing her to rise to the occasion on a daily basis. She wouldn't change her circumstances for the world.

As the helicopter landed on the helipad, Chey unbuckled, preparing to disembark. Resting the headset on the seat, she accepted a hand down and ducked the spinning rotors on her way to the waiting limousine. Thunder rumbled in the distance. A storm was coming, rolling in from the west. She could smell rain on the air, feel the electric charge against her skin.

Urmas waited inside the car, dressed as immaculately as ever, a folder sitting on his thighs.

"Urmas," Chey said as she settled into the seat. "It couldn't wait ten minutes for the ride to Kallaster?"

Urmas smiled. "Your first priority will be to see your children straightaway. I figured I'd better use every spare second I can."

Chey laughed and couldn't deny it—he

was right. Her first order of business once in the castle was to head straight for her kids. "Okay. Lay it on me then, Urmas. Let's see if we can get all the business out of the way before the limousine stops at the steps."

Urmas opened the folder. "Now then…"

In the back of her mind, Chey sent up a quick prayer that the men's travel wouldn't be affected by the oncoming storm.

Chapter Five

Sander had no great love for the hinterlands. There were fewer trees, unexpected ravines hidden by brush that made walking treacherous, and little in the way of beauty this far from the greenbelt. Driving wasn't an option unless one wanted to risk crashing every fifty yards or so. The terrain was too uneven, with boulders hiding behind innocuous looking brush and ancient, dried up creeks that wreaked havoc on suspension systems. Horses were a better option, although if a mount got spooked by the myriad number of creepy-crawlies that inhabited the land, then the risk of an accident increased exponentially should the steed bolt across the unpredictable terrain.

So it was they chose to go on foot from the drop off point. The helicopter got them within five miles of the border, which wasn't a hard delineation but rather a general area that they navigated by GPS. Laden with hiking gear tucked into backpacks and thick walking sticks, Sander set out with Mattias and Leander just as the storm let loose its first drops of rain. There was more to come, Sander knew. The weather report for the area had deteriorated marginally before they'd departed the stronghold. Sander chose to press on anyway. A little rain never hurt anyone.

Attired in camouflage that matched the surrounding terrain, with a hat to block either sun or rain, Sander led the way forward, picking the path of least resistance closer to their destination. In truth, if there *were* trespassers this close to the border, they might encounter them anywhere from this point on. In this desolation, there weren't fences or other barriers to entry. A person could travel overland—for days upon days—and penetrate either country. Armed with two handguns and one rifle, he felt confident the three of them could take on any adversaries they might meet.

Unless Konstantine had been right all along.

After two miles, Sander guided their path parallel to the border, stopping every few hours to use binoculars for a better view across the hinterlands. No one spotted anything suspicious. No small encampments, no out of the ordinary colors, no walking bodies. The rain remained steady throughout, not quite a downpour but more than a sprinkle. Despite that winter had not set in, Sander noted the temperature slowly falling into the low forties, then into the high thirties. They were a few degrees from snow. The rain turned to sleet that pinged off the camouflage like darts.

When the gloom took a turn toward darkness, Sander called a halt for the night. It would do them no good to announce their presence to any night crawlers by spearing flashlight beams across the landscape. As a team, the trio set up a compact tent and ate a hasty dinner of dried beef and trail mix. One man remained on watch while the other two slept, taking turns through the night. This was no more hardship than any other mission they had been on, and in some ways, better than most. Camping out in the middle of nowhere under a storm allowed Sander to have a much needed break from the demands of his position. Out here, where there were no phones, no meetings, no walls, he could just be. During his turn at watch, he sat five feet from the tent with his arms around his drawn up knees, weapon loaded and ready in the holster under his jacket.

Lightning flashed against the inky sky, followed a minute later by deep rolling thunder.

In the morning they broke camp and set out once more, again besieged by the weather. Rain fell harder and the temperature remained right around forty. Mattias marked their progress by GPS— when they could get it to work.

At midday the rain eased to a sprinkle, and then stopped altogether. Clouds still rolled across the sky, an endless procession of patchy white and pewter. It reminded Sander of a witches brew, with frothy peaks and roiling darkness. More rain was not out of the question.

They halted for a break, setting their packs on the ground to scan the area with binoculars. The hinterlands stretched as far as the eye could see. It was as if man had never encroached on this barren terrain, so empty was it of human life. Sander saw no signs that anyone had passed through here in decades. No bits of trash, no leftover campfire rings, no discarded water bottles.

Just before night claimed the land, the men set up camp again.

"I haven't seen anything suspicious at all," Sander said once the tent was up. "Not that we've covered the entire border, but this was generalized to be the most expedient area for anyone to come across if they meant to penetrate our territory, at least as a marching army, and there hasn't been sign of a single remnant of humans."

"I agree," Mattias said as he picked out a slab of beef from a waterproof bag. "Although I think you're right. I say we have the helicopter grab us in the morning and drop us another two hundred miles further down the border. Keep spot checking areas."

It would have been so much easier for the military to conduct pass-overs, Sander thought, except bringing aircraft that close to the border might increase tensions between countries. At some point, the aircraft would ping on their neighbor's radar and Sander wouldn't risk any kind of conflict. Besides, at that altitude, one might miss the smaller signs of humanity passing through the terrain.

Good soldiers wouldn't leave huge, blatant signs of their presence. That's why they were on foot, hunting up subtle signs in the brush.

"That's what we'll do, then." Sander was on board with the suggestions.

For the next three days, that was how the three men searched. They covered perhaps ten miles on foot, were airlifted to a different drop spot, and started over again. As hard as they searched, they never found one indication that an army had passed through, large or small, or even smaller indications that anyone had stopped to camp.

On the sixth day, the trio climbed aboard the helicopter for the last time. They had been gone longer than expected, but Sander now had a better idea of what parts of his border with Russia looked like. There were no troops amassed as far as he could see. Flanked on both other sides by different countries, there was no way foreign militants had penetrated those borders to come at him from the interior.

As the chopper headed for home, Sander received an update from Urmas via the co-pilot.

Konstantine had arrived overnight and

awaited Sander's presence.

Another attack, according to the king, had occurred on Imatra's soil.

* * *

Chey stared down into her oldest son's face. Elias wore his impatience and growing frustration on the surface, his features beginning to skew toward discontent. He was as tall as her hip now, growing like a weed and ever so much his father's son.

"He's due home any second, Elias. I promise, as soon as he gets here and cleans up, he'll come to see you. Why don't you shoot another basket?"

"But *Mooom...*"

"No buts." Chey shooed Elias across the half court, bouncing the basketball on the shiny surface so that her son had to catch it. The activity room, as Chey called it, was a converted ballroom on the lower floor of Kallaster castle. An older ballroom not on as grand a scale as the other two. It was more than suitable for the half court, ballet bar, miniature bowling lanes and two trampolines. Two, one for the kids and one for her and Sander when they challenged the kids to see who could do the most forward flips in a minute. One wall had been converted into a rock climb, replete with safety harnesses and a soft mat in case a cable broke. In the dead of winter, during the most severe snowstorms, it gave the children something active to do.

Emily ran in and out of a small pretend kitchen, busy 'baking' pies and cookies and washing dishes. As tomboyish as she could sometimes be, Emily was nevertheless driven to play dollhouse on a regular basis. And, by all accounts, their daughter had grown into a spitting image of Chey. Long dark hair, lively blue eyes, same shaped face.

Erick, the youngest, toddled through a tunnel maze, giggling and laughing and entertaining himself. At least they were preoccupied for now. Chey wasn't sure how much longer it would last. The kids were restless and wanted their daddy. Most of Sander's trips these days lasted no more than three to four days. He always came back to see the children and spend time if he had to leave soon after.

"What, no surprise parties, no big welcome cake?" Sander's voice boomed from the doorway.

Startled, Chey turned to see Sander,

still in his camouflage gear and muddy boots, throw his arms wide to the kids. He crouched, preparing for impact. Elias was already running. Emily squealed and deserted her four layer (plastic) cake in favor of following in Elias's footsteps. Sander snatched each in an arm and lifted them while he laughed, pecking adoring kisses to their cheeks.

The giggling, laughing Erick heard the commotion and tried to climb his way out of the tunnel, forgetting which way was out. An ear piercing squall let everyone know that Erick was not a happy little prince.

Chey bit back amusement and started over to help her son find his way free.

"I'll get him," Sander said, pausing to kiss Chey on the mouth before stalking the maze of tunnels. "Fee Fi Fo Fum, I smell the blood of....Erick!" he boomed. Elias and Emily, arms around his neck, encouraged the 'giant' to find the baby.

If only she had her camera. Chey groused at the lack, licking the taste of Sander off her lip. He smelled like the outdoors, like the wild. She loved seeing him wrestle with the kids, which he promptly did once he'd extracted Erick from the tunnel. The four rolled around on one of the mats, lavishing love on each other. Sander's booming laugh rang out again and again, sending a warm, fuzzy feeling through her belly. If there was anything she loved more than Sander, it was seeing him and their kids together. Sander was a father above all else, putting the children before his own needs and wants.

Clearly, since he'd apparently come straight here from the hinterlands without changing or showering first.

Finally, a half hour into the third tickle and wrestling match, Chey broke up the fun. She sent Elias off with the assistants for writing lessons and had Emily and Erick prepared for naps. Once the kids were gone, Chey faced Sander, reaching up to tug on the bill of his hat. His hair stuck out the bottom, no longer contained by a band.

"Two or three days, you said..." She wasn't, *couldn't,* be angry. That didn't mean she would pass up the opportunity to tease him.

He flashed a boyish grin and pulled her close by the hips. "I thought about you every second."

"Every second you weren't scouring the landscape for the enemy, you mean?"

74

Chey snorted.

He rumbled and bent to kiss her.

Chey didn't care if he needed a shower, she kissed him until she felt his body respond. Then, *then* she released him. She knew their time was short. He had a meeting to get to.

"Everything go all right while I was gone?" he asked, escorting her to the doors.

Chey walked alongside as they headed to the upper floors and their bedroom suite. "Yes. The only major development was Konstantine's arrival late last evening. I haven't spoken to him yet."

"Urmas said he wishes to speak only to me. We'll see what he wants. I don't know if he'll stay another evening. If he does, we'll arrange a formal dinner later." Sander broke away once they were in their suite. He stripped out of his clothes, boots first and pants next.

Chey watched from her spot in a cushy chair. There was never a moment when she would tire of watching her husband move through the mundane task of undressing. She adored every hard inch, from his muscled thighs to his rigid stomach to the bulge of his biceps.

He caught her looking and quirked a

knowing smile her way.

Chey wagged her brows, and didn't hesitate when he ticked his head toward the shower, a silent invitation to join him. She made a show of stripping out of her own clothes, too, heat sparking through her system at the blatant way he looked her over. Like he meant to claim her as thoroughly as he had before he left.

And he did. Against the shower wall, with striking possessive intensity that rendered Chey weak-kneed and breathless. She knew by the pressure of his fingertips that he'd branded her with their imprint. Tomorrow, and the next day, there would be proof of this tryst on her skin.

In the aftermath, she leisurely dragged a soapy cloth over all the muscles she so admired, and even let him wash her hair with a vanilla-raspberry scented shampoo that he stroked into her scalp with skilled fingertips. He had a way about it, a slow massage that made Chey want to melt into the floor. That he whispered endearments and risque things in her ear only added to the allure.

Once they were both clean, Chey snatched a towel from the rack and dried off. In recent weeks, desiring change, she had lopped off six inches of hair. Instead of hanging more than halfway down her back, it now hung even with the top of her shoulder blades and was much less hassle to deal with. While rubbing the towel through the damp strands, she said, "You probably shouldn't have made your guest wait so long."

Sander ran a towel along his thighs with quick, efficient strokes. "Perhaps Konstantine should have given us more warning. Or, even come here to speak face to face the first time. He can wait an extra fifteen minutes."

"It's been more like an hour." Chey couldn't help but smile.

"And it may be another hour if you keep looking at me like that." He arched his brows and tossed the towel to the hamper when he was through. Winking, he cut away for the closet.

Chey reined in a sassy retort. If she challenged Sander, even in play, he might keep his word to make Konstantine wait another hour. Not that *she* would mind. She was anxious to find out what the king had to say, however, so she ceased flirting with her husband and, taking her time since she wasn't attending this particular visitation, began the process of readying for a dinner in which they might or might not have a new guest.

She hoped, for the sake of everyone involved, that the visiting king wanted something other than requests for Latvala to engage with Imatra in battle.

Chapter Six

Sander descended to the main floor, giving the steel gray suit a final tug. His fingers smoothed the length of the deep blue tie as Urmas fell into step at his side and updated him on the latest. Which happened to be nothing he didn't already know. Konstantine refused to speak with anyone but Sander, one on one, regarding an immediate matter. Guards for both sovereigns waited just outside the king's parlor, standing watch despite the already heavy security.

Sander entered the austere chamber which continued a more medieval theme rather than a palatial one. Instead of gilt trimmings and white walls, the colors were warm and rich, with heavy wood tables, brocade and chenille chairs, and paintings—fittingly enough—depicting Latvala's ancestors locked in battle with their adversary. Once upon a time, Latvala's warriors had fought for, died for, the independence of the country.

Konstantine paced near the tall fireplace, where a small fire currently burned, looking at photographs with his hands clasped behind his back. He had dressed for the occasion: sharp black suit, polished shoes, crisp white shirt and a dark cloak that fell from his shoulders in dramatic fashion. Like Sander, he wore his brown hair tied back at the nape. In his early thirties, Konstantine kept himself in decent shape, although Sander discerned a softness in Konstantine's physique that suggested he did not do much in the way of serious activity. Here was a king who preferred to pass his rule down from the safety of his throne, rarely exerting himself unless it was on his terms and for fun. He had lean features and a sharp jaw that many women—if rumors were true—found irresistible. Sander had met Konstantine several times, in passing, but had never desired to make pacts or become allies.

"Welcome to Kallaster, King Konstantine," Sander said, standing on ceremony in these initial greetings.

Konstantine turned from the mantel and fixed Sander with a somewhat serious stare. "Dare. If I may call you that--"

"You have already, have you not?" Sander interrupted. He stood rather than take a seat, since Konstantine did not appear ready to relax any time soon. 'Dare', his nickname from childhood, was not typically used so casually by other members of regal society. Sander was sure Konstantine knew it.

"Did your people not tell you that I have come on urgent business? I have been waiting hours."

"My apologies. Perhaps if you had given *some* kind of notice, you would not have had to wait. I was not anywhere near Pallan Island when you arrived." Sander wanted to tell Konstantine that he was lucky Sander had returned when he did. Otherwise, the king might have been forced to return to Imatra empty handed.

"The situation in Imatra has escalated since my last *request* to you. There has been another, larger attack. A military outpost was completely decimated by a Russian contingent. We lost ten more men. Not only that, I have received missives from a Russian commander that unless I allow Imatra to be absorbed into Russia's fold, they will wage war on my country." Konstantine reached into the liner of his jacket, withdrew an envelope, and crossed the room to offer it out to Sander.

Tensing when Konstantine reached for the inside of the jacket, Sander eased when nothing more sinister than a letter appeared. His instincts were working overtime. Accepting the envelope, he withdrew a folded letter and scanned the contents. He was not pleased at the news that another, larger skirmish had occurred. Committing the Russian commander's name assigned to the letter to memory, which did indeed state that Imatra had thirty days to respond to Russia's demands, Sander slipped the letter into the envelope and handed it back to Konstantine. Despite the letter and the newest attack, Sander was not convinced that it was time to send in troops. This situation was deteriorating rapidly and he needed to consider every angle, every option. If he'd learned anything in his position as king, it was to never act without first determining that he had all his facts in order.

"Tell the commander you do not accept the terms and that you will release the demands to the media. Pressure from the international community will force Russia's hand and, in this instance, I believe they'll back down," Sander said.

Konstantine accepted the envelope, his jaw tightening at Sander's reply. "I do not think you understand what's at stake here. You do not see the bigger picture. If I acquiesce to their demands, then their next target will be Somero and after that, Latvala. They want control of the coast and we're standing in their way. We, all three of us, will lose everything if we do not make a strong defense here and now. The situation is immediate and dire. There is no time to waste."

"So you want me to send a few troops to help protect your border, which will result in more skirmishes and more deaths, when you might stop any advance at all if you simply expose Russia's agenda to the world." Sander watched what appeared to be fear cross Konstantine's features.

"It will do nothing except perhaps stall their attack by a few weeks, if that. They have made their agenda perfectly clear. They are coming, Dare, it's right there in black and white. It's in the blood on the ground of my country. Men have already given their lives." Konstantine paced away from Sander, sliding the envelope into the interior pocket once more. He paused and turned to look back. "I'm not asking for a few troops. I'm not even asking for your whole army. I'm suggesting we come together to fight the threat as one. At least we stand a better chance."

"So in essence, you *are* asking for my entire army," Sander countered.

Konstantine lifted his chin an inch. "No, you misunderstand. I mean to merge Imatra and Latvala into one country."

* * *

The ludicrous idea earned a bark of laughter from Sander. "Merge our countries? Have you lost your mind? And I suppose you'll reign supreme over us all, perhaps even delegating your siblings to take over my castles for the better good. Hm? Commandeer my armies, raid my vaults. You cannot be serious."

Konstantine frowned. "You take this too lightly. Who else do you think will come to our aid? And those countries that do will ask for much in return. Better that we band together so we will at least have a fighting chance."

Sander couldn't believe Konstantine's nerve. Either the man was attempting to do the same thing to Latvala that he claimed the Russian's were trying to do to Imatra, or he honestly saw no other way out of his perceived predicament.

"Let me play your little game for a moment. Say we *do* merge. What of Somero, which sits smack between Latvala and Imatra?" Sander paced a few feet through the room but never took his eyes off Konstantine.

"We approach King Thane with the same offer. Three become one. Imagine the strength we will have then," Konstantine said.

"I know Thane's reputation well enough to know that he will have the same answer as I do. What then? We cannot 'merge' with an entire country between us. What are your plans in that scenario?" Sander was losing patience with such nonsensical talk. He suspected Konstantine might be up to some other mischief here, or that his agenda was not as pure as he wanted everyone else to believe.

"We *make* them listen," Konstantine said.

"You mean invade them, as you say Russia is threatening to do to you. No, absolutely not. My kingdom will not be a part of your sudden desire for take over.

You dress your suggestions up in urgency, as matters of life and death, but where is the proof? I have seen a few photos—of which are suspect—and a letter I have not even confirmed is real. Do you have footage of the latest attack? Latvala will not 'merge' with any other country and that is my final decision."

"I have heard that about you. That you will allow your country to fall—which it nearly did with the scandals so many years ago—before you will take the action that best benefits Latvala. *I* say it's the fault of having a half blooded king as sovereign, a man whose iron fisted control knows no bounds. You've got the throne, even though it does not belong to you, and you will not give it up for anything. It may mean the death of your people but you're careless of consequence so long as you remain king. Here is my prediction: your arrogance will be your downfall." Konstantine, full of agitated tension, pivoted toward the door.

Sander stepped between the stalking king and the exit. If Konstantine wanted out, he would have to move Sander to do it. "It is not the mark of a king to threaten those who do not abide by his word, but the mark of a tyrant. Consider yourself warned, King Konstantine. I perceive a threat in your statement and should you move to strike against me, to—how did you put it—*make me listen,* I will not hesitate to defend *my* country with all due force. In your selfish attempt to overthrow two countries, your own may be attacked by more than one enemy at a time."

"This is not a take over. Have you not been listening? We are about to go to war! You've seen the letter first hand and yet you still balk when I offer a solution—the only solution—to give us a chance to win. Your children's lives--"

Sander grabbed Konstantine by the throat and shoved him against the nearest wall. Decorum and etiquette be damned. Nose to nose, fury getting the better of him, he said, "Do not ever mention my children again. Breathe one word of threat and I will gut you where you stand. Am I understood?"

"Guards!" Konstantine's shout came out as no more than a raspy whisper.

Sander tightened his hold, fingers squeezing hard enough to feel the rapid pulse in Konstantine's neck. "Am. I. Understood?" he repeated, word for word.

"Yes, yes." Konstantine struggled

against the hold, his face turning purple.

Sander released Konstantine's throat but shoved at his shoulder, too angry to be diplomatic about 'escorting' his 'guest' to the door. He opened it and, with Konstantine choking and gasping, followed him into the hall.

All hell was about to break loose.

Chapter Seven

Chey stepped into the main foyer just as a commotion broke out down one of the hallways. She twisted to see what the fuss was about, taking note of the sudden tension that swept through the castle security and the stalking stride of the oncoming men. The red-faced man in the lead, flanked by guards, looked furious. She guessed, by the cut of his clothing and the cloak—which was an odd garment in this day and age—that he must be Konstantine. Sander appeared not far behind, his own face a mask of controlled rage. Several advisors talked over each other to the point Chey could not detect what the problem was.

Clearly, the meeting had not gone well at all.

The group entered the foyer, more of Sander's advisors and guards coming from other hallways, drawn by the upheaval.

"Escort King Konstantine to his

helicopter and see that every man of his goes with him. He will not be staying, nor returning." Sander's command came in a terse, clipped voice that brooked no argument.

Chey darted a look at her husband's face, wondering what had gotten so under his skin. There were few things that could wrest this kind of emotion from him.

Konstantine marched toward the doors, which two guards opened. The king paused at the threshold, backlit by the diffused pall of another overcast day. "You have made a grave mistake. Before this week is through, you will be groveling to take me up on my offer. Mark my words."

"Get him out of here," Sander snarled.

Chey struggled to conceal her surprise. She glanced between kings, with advisors and guards standing in a circle around them, watching the sovereigns trade glares. Konstantine departed with a flourish of his cloak, his men following close behind. A handful of Sander's own security shadowed the men, prepared to follow the king's orders to the end.

"Close the doors," Sander bellowed. "Urmas, arrange a meeting with my brothers and Leander Morgan before the night's end. Get them here, I don't care where they currently are or what they're doing." Sander shot Chey a direct look, holding her eyes for several seconds, before he took to the stairs.

Chey didn't need to be asked twice to follow. She trotted up in Sander's wake as guards, advisors and other staff scattered to the four winds. Sander chose their bedroom suite, much to Chey's surprise, and closed the door once she had stepped inside.

"Sander, what in the world--"

"Konstantine proposed a ludicrous idea to merge our two countries--"

"What?"

"Listen. Just listen. He wants to merge our countries against what he says is a threat of invasion from Russia. His idea is to combine our economies and armies and no doubt, have everything under his absolute rule. I declined, of course, to which he predicted that my 'arrogance' would be my downfall. I did not take it that we would fall to the Russians, but rather to an attack by *him*. As if that would make me change my mind. Then he mentioned something about the children--"

Chey gasped. "He did *what?* Did he

threaten them out right?"

"Not in so many words, but the damage was done by then and I will not allow *any* tyrant to speak on my children while at the same time informing me that I will be groveling to take him up on his offer. You heard him at the door. A king does not make those kinds of statements lightly."

Shocked to her core at the very idea someone might even think of bringing harm to her children, and more understanding now of Sander's foul mood, she said, "Surely he must be talking just to hear himself talk. He can't be serious about a merger between countries. What of Somero? It sits directly between us."

"That's what I said, too, and his answer was to either bring Somero onboard or, in Konstantine's words, *make them listen.* He double speaks and I trust a man who does that about as much as I trust a snake. I want you to be extra alert. Don't go riding alone or take the kids out to the shore without heavy escort. If you go to the mainland, be sure to be within a guard's sight at all times. Double check everything. If someone gives you a message from me, and you think it's suspicious at all, then call me directly. We're safer on the island than anywhere, so if you will, stay close until this is resolved."

"Have we come to this? Is it really this critical this fast?" Dismayed that their years of semi-peace had been shattered in one short afternoon, Chey nevertheless took every word to heart. She had learned long ago that Sander had excellent battle instincts and she would do as he asked.

"Yes. Which tells me there is a timeline of sorts, and that already, a few things have not gone according to Konstantine's plan. He is under some kind of pressure, either from a real foe or something else entirely."

"Could it be that he's telling the truth, and that the Russians are making a move?" she asked.

"Nothing is ever out of the realm of possibility. Konstantine swears that if Imatra falls, Somero and Latvala are next. I have my doubts about that but above all else, we need to keep everyone safe." Sander adjusted a cuff, giving the material a tight tug. "I saw nothing in the hinterlands to suggest anyone has been there in decades. Not one Russian, spy or scavenger in sight."

"You didn't have time to check the entire border, right? What if they are gathered at a point you didn't look?" Chey asked. "Can't you fly close enough to the border to at least cover more ground, getting a better idea if there are pockets of men clustered near Latvala territory?"

"*If* Russia is preparing for a ground assault, flying that close to the border may provoke them. If they are not, then a fly-over may bring us to their attention, put us on their proverbial radar. I'll send scouts to the hinterlands to keep an eye on things, but for now, I prefer to act as if we know nothing about what's going on. Until I can learn more, and see what Konstantine might or might not do, I want to remain as we are. Remember, if there *is* any kind of attack on our soil, get yourself and the kids into the air as quickly as possible. The main runway in Kalev isn't the only runway the jet can take off from, so arrange it with Urmas beforehand."

Kalev, the capital on the mainland, was the home of the biggest airport in the country. Chey knew there were others though, as Sander had said, and filed that information away to take care of after this conversation was done. "All

94

right. I will. Are you going to make an announcement to the public?"

"No. I want all this kept as quiet as possible. I've fought too hard to bring this country back together after my father and Paavo's antics to scare the population with talk of possible invasion or attack."

"If you don't say anything at all, and Konstantine does the unthinkable, or the Russians, then won't the people blame you for not giving them any warning?"

"They might. But I'll take that chance. This happens all the time, withholding sensitive information from the population. There have been numerous 'almost wars' that only a select few in humanity will ever know about. It comes down to what is safer for the people at the time. If I announce there might be an attack, and the population rushes out and clears the shelves of food in five hours, there will be citizens—many thousands of them—who missed out and will go hungry. Arguments and robberies may escalate, and things may even deteriorate into civil unrest. I could be judged harshly on the backside of that for scaring the public unnecessarily. I just don't have enough proof yet that Konstantine will actually take the next step. He could be scare mongering for all I know. What I *will* do is take every precaution I can and maybe even send in a spy or two. For now, we hold tight." Sander set a hand on her shoulder and squeezed, then drew Chey into a hug.

"It's very complicated, all the things you have to consider." It made Chey's head spin. There were no clear cut lines, no transcript to tell anyone what to do.

"It's always complicated. Just like the situation with my father and my brother. We'll have these things crop up for the rest of our lives. Now," he said, pressing a quick kiss to her forehead. "I have things to do. It would be prudent to pack a few bags for you and the kids, just in case."

"I will. Let me know what's going on and if you have to leave the castle." Chey didn't want Sander to leave without a final goodbye.

For all she knew, it might be their last.

* * *

Between leaving Chey and reaching the conference room where his brothers and Leander waited, Sander stopped four different times to give orders to specific people. Urmas, advisors, military personnel, castle guards. He left no stone unturned. Konstantine's threats might amount to nothing—and he hoped that was the case—but he thought it wise to be prepared for the worst.

Entering the downstairs conference room, Sander found everyone present and waiting.

"You cannot believe the things I'm hearing," Mattias said first.

"I second that," Leander chimed in.

"Is it true? There may be an attack on Latvala soil?" Gunnar added.

Sander shut the door. In as precise terms as he could manage, he caught his brothers and Leander up to speed. He left nothing out. Not the implied threats—or his perception of them—nor Konstantine's assertion that Sander would be groveling to take up the offer before the week was out.

"So as a precaution, I've put Chey on alert and they're ready to leave here should the situation arise," Sander said in conclusion. Mattias looked thoughtful, Gunnar was frowning, and Leander had begun to pace the room.

"Usually when something like this happens, you hear about it through word of mouth," Leander finally said. "I've asked around, been listening to the whispers of people who should be in the know, and there's very little information. Either Russia is keeping a very tight lid on this, or Konstantine has some other agenda. He *may* be attempting an overthrow—but in a very unusual and strange way. Trying to get you to submit, then once he's publicly merged the two countries, there's an assassination attempt on you, Sander, so he's in control of both armies. With Imatra and Latvala on either side of Somero, he could put a lot more pressure on Somero to either join or go down in flames."

"That's impossible. It's so bold and so aggressive it seems no man would dare try it," Gunnar said.

"Nothing is *impossible* Gunnar," Mattias added. "Would you have ever thought your own brother would order Sander's entire convoy blown up?"

A brief hush fell over the room until Gunnar quietly said, "No."

"Or," Mattias continued, " Konstantine *did* receive those threats and that letter is real. He may be the type who is easily spooked and his gut reaction was to send word to Sander for help, then to come here with erratic threats because while we're conjecturing what Konstantine *might* do to Sander, it's a near certainty that there's a hit out on Konstantine as we speak and he's in desperate fear for his own life."

"Has his rule ever been challenged that we know of?" Leander asked.

Sander considered all the options. Mattias's assertion that Konstantine's own life might be in jeopardy had not occurred to him. "He took the throne last year. Honestly, I haven't been paying extreme attention to those kinds of details." He'd been busy trying to salvage his own country and secure his reign as king.

"I don't think so. But I'll have someone look into it," Mattias said.

"He could have approached all this in a better way," Sander muttered.

"Absolutely. Some men, as I mentioned, are easily spooked when the word assassination comes up. But I can also see Leander's take on it, too. There's no way to know for sure what's going on. I think the right call, in either circumstance, was to decline and remain on notice," Mattias said to Sander.

"Do you want me to get into his house?" Leander asked.

Sander glanced at Leander. The man, who was so skilled at getting in and out of tricky situations, could probably learn more in ten minutes inside Konstantine's stronghold than they could in a week of prying from the outside. But Leander was a father now, too, and had a wife who happened to be Chey's best friend. Not only that, the mission was extremely risky. If Leander was caught, a spy in Konstantine's own house, he could be tried and executed. And, Sander reminded himself, it would give Konstantine an excuse to attack. A flimsy excuse, but nevertheless.

"No. I won't risk your life. Let's do some more digging over the next week and see what happens. *If* Konstantine is attacked again, let's find out the who and why of it this time. Someone out in the 'community' has to know something. And if there's an attempt on his life—or mine —we'll have a better idea what's going on. If you can lean on our contacts to listen in on a phone call or two, Leander, that would be even better. Get the information from a safe distance." Sander rubbed his chin in consideration and assessed each man's reaction. Mattias nodded, on board with the decision. Leander looked mildly disappointed not to have an aggressive mission like spying to tackle, but Sander knew he wouldn't go against the order to stand down. Gunnar was still frowning, hands on his hips.

Relieved to see that everyone was in agreement with the tentative plan, Sander breathed easier. This was becoming a tenuous situation and, without knowing more details, there was every chance that he could be making a wrong decision. He didn't want to risk anyone's life until there was no other choice.

The 'community', a network of undercover agents, spies and men committed to the safety of others should be able to shed some light on the truth. Sander and his brethren were a part of that community, a group who dedicated their time, energy and resources to try and keep the oft threatened members of the elite alive. Assassination attempts happened more frequently than people realized. Or, at the very least, were talked about behind closed doors.

If he and his men could get the information they needed without triggering a war, all the better.

Chapter Eight

Flickers of candlelight crawled up the stone walls flanking the double-sized, claw footed tub. Another storm had moved across Latvala later in the evening, knocking out the power and bringing an end to the relentless schedule of meetings. Chey, neck deep in sudsy water, leaned further back against Sander's chest. The kids were long in their beds and rain still fell in sheets past the windows, affording her and Sander a little alone time. Sander might have worked through the night if Chey hadn't intervened and requested his presence in their suite.

The bath—well. That was an unexpected bonus after she'd pried all the information she could out of him regarding his meetings and plans. Frothy suds decorated the wavy surface of the water as well as any exposed skin, and she cupped her hands around a peak to squish between her fingers. Sander's hands were on her body, gliding around her ribs, over her breasts and down her stomach in slow circles. The rough callouses on his palms felt especially good when he grazed them across her nipples.

"I have a hypothetical question for you," she said in a low voice. The water rippled around her updrawn knees.

"Hm?" Sander rumbled the noise close to her ear.

Chey shuddered, nearly forgetting what she wanted to ask. "What would you do if someone assassinated Konstantine and attempted to take Imatra?" Since the Russians had not been identified positively, Chey left the threat vague.

"That depends. Have we received a direct threat? Does it appear like the invaders will turn to Somero and Latvala next? What does the next in line to the throne of Imatra want? In this case, Aleksi, Konstantine's brother, might *want* to align with the invader."

"Why would anyone want to do that?" Chey asked.

"I don't know Aleksi any better than I know Konstantine, but perhaps he may think it's safer for Imatra to be absorbed by a larger country, especially if he is allowed to retain a seat of power and make decisions directly regarding the welfare of the people. If that's the case, then Latvala should not interfere. I wouldn't send troops unless the situation became dire and I knew other countries were standing with us, not against us. We don't have enough men and women to fight an army as large as Russia's—*if* that is who is behind the skirmishes." Sander's hands flattened over Chey's ribs, massaging down to her hips.

"I can understand that strategy. Do you go over all this in your head a million times? I'm not even king and I can't seem to quit thinking about all the variables," she admitted.

"Yes," he said in a quiet voice. "Everything hinges on something else. Who is doing what, how many lives each action will cost, and what the best outcome will be. I do not take sending troops into battle lightly. If *we* were being invaded under the same circumstances, then I would call upon the allies we have and fight back. Being absorbed into a super-power does not interest me."

"It's like you knew I was going to ask that next, although I was pretty sure I knew the answer beforehand." Chey tickled her fingertips up the muscled length of Sander's forearms, reveling in the sinewy strength.

"I know you better than you think I do," he murmured near her ear.

"I suspect you're right. Would *you* fight if it came down to that?" she asked.

"As much as I would want to...no. Not only would I be a distraction for the men, I would be a prime target for abduction or assassination. And if we needed more help, more troops from our allies, I have to be able to get in contact with other people in power to request aid. Doing that on the battlefield would prove difficult at best."

"I hope it doesn't come to that. For Imatra, or for us."

"I hope not, either. The day after tomorrow I'm going to travel to Somero and meet with the king. I shouldn't be gone longer than a handful of hours," he said.

"Is it safe?"

"As safe as it ever can be. So far, we have no proof the Russians are doing anything. There are no troops at the border. We'll find out if Thane is receiving threats as well to help guide our own decisions."

"Since you have to take the jet and fly

out on the mainland, why don't I pack the kids and we'll stay at Ahtissari castle until you get back? It's only a half day or so. You know how much Elias loves to take the helicopter rides from the island to the mainland." She smiled, remembering her oldest son's penchant for flying.

"That's fine. We won't be there long."

Chey drew slow, swirly designs on the thick muscle of Sander's thighs. Thinking. "We've had a good reprieve these last few years regarding attacks or subterfuge. I know it hasn't been easy recovering from the last event," she meant Paavo and the attacks that nearly tore Latvala apart, "but at least we weren't under direct threat of war or situations like this. I guess I got a little complacent."

"Konstantine may back down and things will smooth out again. All of this might amount to nothing more than a few tense conversations before it's over. Something else will come up of course, it always does, but perhaps we'll have another handful of peaceful years in between."

"That sounds excellent. And I know what we can do to wile away the hours in

the meantime," she said, dragging her
hands higher up this thighs.

Sander said, "I like the way you think."

* * *

The country of Somero, roughly half
the size of Latvala's land mass, had quite
a lot of commerce and residential areas
packed into a relatively small region.
Toward the coastal areas, which was
where Sander's private jet touched down,
he could see endless streets and grids
that made up the main city. It appeared
that many more citizens chose to live
closer to the cities than toward the
interior of the territory, either by choice
or by design. Latvala's main cities were
also busy, but his people preferred to
spread out into the countryside a little
more.

From the private airstrip, a limousine
escorted Sander and four guards to the
main palace, which sat apart from the
city by several miles on its own road, on
its own high plateau, with a stunning
view of distant buildings. Not of the scale
of the Ahtissari family seat by far, but
resplendent nevertheless. The palace
itself sprawled across the landscape,

three floors high, with spires and peaks of a more baroque design than the castles that decorated his homeland.

After two separate security check points, the limousine pulled into a breezeway surrounded by the palace walls, where Sander entered the building by a private, elaborate entrance. With his guards at his heels, Sander strode the polished floors behind an official escort, bypassing stunning works of art and architecture. Vases half as tall as Sander decorated niches in the walls and alabaster sculptures stood on small pedestals, beautiful and unique. Arriving at an impressively carved archway, the double doors already open, Sander ordered his security to remain at the entrance and strolled into the large room after the escort gestured him inside. The doors closed quietly in Sander's wake.

Bookshelves stuffed with an endless array of tomes lined three of four walls, creating a comfortable atmosphere to go with the elegant furniture in colors that enhanced the dark wood of the bookcases. A floor to ceiling fireplace sat to the far right, carved with cherubs holding vases of ivy.

King Thane Ascher strode through a

separate door on the opposite side of the room, easily as tall as Sander and just as broad through the shoulder. He wore a suit of silver with darker gray pinstripes and a navy accented tie. His eyes were the lightest hazel, leaning toward green rather than brown, and fixed on Sander as he smiled and crossed through the maze of furniture, one hand extending just ahead of his arrival. The dark layers of his hair, perhaps as long as Sander's, had been pulled back into a neat tail at his nape.

"King Ahtissari, welcome to Ascher House."

"Thank you for accepting my visit. It's a wonder we haven't met up before this on a more personal level," Sander said, clasping Thane's hand for a shake. He made direct eye contact, then released the man's hand. He unbuttoned his formal beige suit coat and whisked the edges to the sides. Coupled with matching beige slacks and a cream colored shirt, Sander had chosen lighter themed attire rather than austere black and white.

Sander had only met Thane in passing at one gala or another and never in an official manner. Caught up in the troubles and strife that Paavo created, Sander hadn't reached out to his neighbors very often. He recalled that Thane had come into power some four years before when his father died after a fall from his horse.

"Indeed, Sander—may I call you Sander? Please call me Thane," the king said, with a distinct rasp to his voice. He gestured to an arrangement of seating that allowed the men to recline and speak without craning their necks, a more informal way of conversing than sitting at a conference table.

"Absolutely." Sander settled into the cushions, assessing Thane's demeanor and reactions. The man seemed astute and intuitive. He almost reminded Sander of a medieval knight, though for what reason specifically, Sander couldn't say. "The reason I stated for my visit is not the real reason I'm here," Sander said, moving into the subject rather quickly.

Thane's brows arched in curiosity. "Not a state visit, then?"

"No. I'm here to ask if you've heard from our neighbor to the north, and whether or not there has been any strange activity along your border with Russia." Sander observed a flicker of surprise in Thane's eyes.

110

"Heard from Konstantine? I have not. And no, there have been no reports of incursions from any direction on Somero soil. May I ask why?" Thane, appearing intrigued, sat forward and rested his elbows on his thighs.

Sander did not mistake the gleam of interest in Thane's eyes. His reaction seemed genuine. "Konstantine appealed to me last week for use of my troops. He sent pictures of a supposed Russian incursion in his territory near the border. After examining the evidence, I informed him via our advisors that I would not be sending troops to Imatra. He visited me in person several days ago with a stunning proposition, which I also declined. Konstantine implied I, and my country, would grovel within the week to accept his offer."

Thane's features shifted from intrigue to thinly veiled surprise. "Those are harsh words. Did he use them exactly?"

"Yes."

"What was the stunning proposition, if it's not intrusive to ask. This is the first I have heard of any of it."

Sander detected no lies in Thane's reply or his demeanor. That was not solid proof the king told the truth, but it eased some of Sander's hesitancy to discuss the more personal aspects of the meeting with Konstantine. He said, "Konstantine proposed Imatra and Latvala 'merge' together. Become one country. And when I asked him how that logistically would work out with Somero, he said he will ask you to come on board as well."

Thane stood up from his seat, a sound of disbelief rumbling from his chest. "What kind of ridiculous notion is that? To *merge?* Did Konstantine happen to mention who would rule this illustrious joining of nations?" Thane asked with knowing snort.

"Of course not, but I'll give you one guess who *thinks* he will reign over all three territories, and his name is not Sander or Thane." Sander leaned back in his seat, inwardly pleased at Thane's indignant reaction to the idea that someone would press him to cede power over his country.

"I have heard rumors of Konstantine's poor management since taking the throne last year. There is no way I would begin to consider merging with Imatra, even if he promised that the kings who now reign would still have control of their territories after the 'merger'. He will receive the same answer from me that he received from you."

"There's more," Sander said. He tracked Thane with his eyes, following the king's movements through the room. Thane was agitated over the news, a good sign in Sander's eyes.

"More? He really did overstep, did he not?"

"Indeed. When I asked him what 'we' would do—during a hypothetical question and answer session—should you decline to join forces with 'us', he said he would *make you listen.* I don't know about you, but where I come from, that's an open threat. Somehow, Thane, I do not believe Konstantine is talking about having a conversation."

Thane ceased pacing. The look he sent Sander's way became instantly predatory, gaze gleaming as if to say, *let him come.* "Konstantine might believe because of Somero's smaller size that we are easily defeated, but our soldiers are hardened warriors who will not go down without a fight."

"As are my men. I have put my armies on alert, just in case this isn't all a bunch of hot air. I don't know how far he would take it, but he seemed pretty intent and aggressive with his ideals." Sander felt Thane was a kindred spirit in regards to Konstantine. His gut instinct told him he could trust the dark haired sovereign on all fronts. For a moment, and only a moment, Sander regretted not pursuing a friendship of sorts with Thane.

"I will do the same, just in case." Thane rolled a shoulder, as if he was working out a kink in the muscle. Then he asked, "What made you initially decline to send troops to Imatra? Something off about his story?"

"Not so much the story as the photos. I can't explain it better than to say it looked like a set up. There was a Russian flag—a formal sized flag—beneath a body on the ground. If that was a stealth mission, which by all rights it appears to have been, then why would the Russians carry a giant banner to all but announce who they were to the enemy? It sat wrong with me right off the bat."

"As it should. When was the last time foot soldiers hoisted a flag going into battle? The middle ages, maybe."

"That's exactly the same thing I said." Sander was briefly amused that he and Thane had come to the same conclusion about the flag.

"Do you think he staged the whole thing?"

"I don't know, to be honest with you, Thane. The scenes in the photos just didn't seem...organic to me. Other than the flag, I'm not sure why. Something was off, however. Maybe it happened to be the angle or the time of day or whatever else."

"Did the bodies actually look dead, or were they actors?" Thane asked, still pacing beyond a settee across from Sander.

"They did look dead. Though I suppose someone could fake bullet wounds and blood. If he *did* fake the photos—why? Why would he do such a thing? What does he stand to gain?" Sander wanted to see if Thane came to some of the same conclusions he and Mattias and Leander had.

Thane tipped his head left and right in contemplation. "He might have staged it to gain sympathy from you, of course, so that you would feel more compelled to give up your troops or join forces with him." Thane paused to cut a look directly at Sander. "You have stepped up your personal security, I hope. Because honestly, I see a strike against *you* should Latvala become one with Imatra."

"I have, yes. You came to the same conclusions my men and I did, which makes me believe we're not far off the mark. We have increased security all around." Sander paused, then added, "And after this visit, I hope you do the same."

"I will. To say thank you for coming with this information seems inadequate and trite, but thank you nevertheless."

"You're welcome. I hope you--" Sander jerked in surprise when a distant *boom* shook the windows of the palace. For a moment, Sander thought they were experiencing an earthquake. His gaze met Thane's and then they were both running for the doors, which flew open under a guard's hand.

"Your Majesty!"

Sander and Thane ignored the guard's attempts to guide Thane to a safe room. They darted into the hall, where other guards—including Sander's own—along with members of the palace staff, created a hectic scene of shouting and fleeing.

"Here!" Thane led Sander into a room on the left, where floor to ceiling windows overlooked the acreage beyond the front of the castle all the way into the outskirts of the city.

A plume of black smoke rose from the landscape, close to the silhouettes of buildings that were separate from the taller high rises of the city itself.

"What is that?" Thane shouted to his men. "Status report!"

Sander's guards flanked him on every side, looking out the windows while they conjectured between them in heated whispers over the cause of what appeared to be an explosion.

Another man, this one in a dark suit with a phone to his ear, rushed into the room. "Your Majesty. There's been an attack on the city. A bomb—the reports are just coming in. An entire building has been taken out."

* * *

Thane barked orders to his men, spinning away from the window. "Sander, pardon me--"

"No apologies. Take care of business." Sander didn't need to be pampered or 'seen to' when Thane clearly needed to concentrate on more important things.

A phone rang. A cell phone that one of Sander's men answered with a curt hello. Suddenly, in an urgent voice, he said,

"The Ahtissari family seat has taken a direct hit. Mass casualties, they think it was a bomb..."

The scene took on that slow, surreal quality of a dream. Sander heard the words, but his mind tripped ahead to thoughts of Chey. His children. All waiting for him at the family seat. Possibly dead. His wife, his heirs, put in the crosshairs by an unknown enemy. Or, perhaps, not so unknown.

Sander didn't remember glancing Thane's way, or shoving past the group of people surrounding the kings. The next thing he knew he was running down the long hall, feet pounding the fine, polished floor, the edges of his jacket flapping like the wings of a startled bird. He hit the door to the breezeway like a linebacker, pointing and shouting for the driver to drive. He glimpsed his guards on his heels when he sank into the back seat of the limousine.

"Go, go, go!" he bellowed, even before the doors were shut. He heard his men making calls. To the castles, to advisors, to the military, to the pilot so the jet would be ready for immediate take off.

The limousine sped away from the palace, taking the turns as tight as a limousine could. Sander fumbled for his phone, chest tight with suppressed fear and panic, his fingers missing the key to dial Chey's phone three times before he got it right.

"Come on, come on," he urged, wishing, hoping, praying for her to pick up. To one of his guards, he said, "How bad is it? Put the entire military on the highest alert."

"Already done," one guard said. "Still waiting on status reports."

"Well tell them to hurry up! Is the whole castle gone? One wall? What?" Sander could hardly fathom the horror of flying over Latvala, over his family's stronghold, to see it reduced to nothing but rubble. Knowing his wife and children and hundreds of others he considered family and friends were dead.

No one answered Chey's phone. A sick sensation curled through his stomach. He fought it down, calling up calm in the face of panic. He needed to remain fluid and flexible. Not allow the unknown to paralyze him.

Once the limousine pulled into the airstrip and stopped adjacent to the private jet, Sander departed the vehicle at a run. He crossed the tarmac and loped up the steps. His men were right behind him, phones at their ears, trying to get more information.

Just as he sank into a seat, his phone rang. "Chey?"

"It's me," Mattias said, his voice strained and tense. "Have you heard?"

"Yes. I'm in the jet, about to take off from Somero. Are my kids alive? Chey? Has anyone had contact?"

"Not yet. It's very early. I'm on my way as well with Leander. We should be there within a half an hour, maybe less."

"Was anyone else at the family seat?" Besides the regular staff, advisors and councilmen, which was devastating enough. Sander couldn't wrap his mind around that kind of loss—*if* the explosion had been in the middle of the castle and not outside a wall. Perhaps it wasn't as bad as it seemed. Maybe a chunk of wall was gone and there were really no casualties at all.

"Natalia is still overseas. Gunnar is with Leander and me," Mattias said.

Despite his fear over Chey and his children, he was relieved to hear other immediate members of the royal family were not in harm's way. "Good, good. I want troops sent to the border--"

"I already did. If this *is* a Russian attack, they'll meet resistance on Latvala territory if they try to come over. I've mobilized all the Generals and the staff. It's taken care of."

"Somero was hit, too. While I was there. In the city, not far from Thane's palace." Sander glanced out the small oval window as the jet taxied to the runway and, after a brief pause, picked up speed for take off.

"What? Hit at the same time?"

"Yes. We heard the explosion. It shook the windows, so it was no small device." Which made Sander imagine the same kind of hit on Ahtissari castle. His stomach turned and once more, he forced himself to push away an overwhelming sense of panic. He couldn't be effective or make the right decisions to help his family or country if he was immobilized by fear.

"Do you think this is a coordinated attack by the Russians—or Konstantine?"

"I don't know. I just know there were two attacks within minutes of each other. We need to be prepared for more. Engage the public warning system and arrange for someone to make an announcement. Give as few details as possible and whatever happens, *do not* allow anyone to even mention the Russians. For now, the enemy is unknown." Sander stared out the window as the terrain became smaller and smaller.

"All right."

"Was this a missile, Mattias?"

"We don't know yet. Let me call you right back. We're about to get in the helicopter."

"Stay on the phone. I know it'll be loud and I don't care. I want to know what you see when you get your first glimpse of the castle." Sander waited through the sounds of his brother transferring from the car to the helicopter, and then a small ruckus as Mattias belted himself in and tucked the phone under the cup of the headset against his ear.

"Can you hear me?" Mattias asked.

"For now." The blades in the background grew louder. Sander refused to hang up. He *needed* to know what Mattias saw. Needed to hear that a device had gone off *outside* the castle walls, that there had been a misunderstanding or a mistake.

"We're in the air," Mattias shouted into the phone.

"Good. I can hear you." Barely. But it

was enough. Sander gripped the armrest and sent up prayer after prayer that the explosion wasn't as bad as the one in Somero had seemed. He felt short of breath while he waited; these were some of the most agonizing moments of his life. While the jet brought him closer to Latvala's borders, the helicopter took Mattias closer to the mainland. It only took a few minutes for Mattias to make his first report.

"We just cleared the island. I can see a column of black smoke from here."

Sander couldn't say anything. He couldn't make his tongue shape words.

"A lot of smoke," Mattias added.

The guards in the plane with Sander had grown quiet, either ending their calls or conducting the conversations in voices too low to hear.

Long minutes went by where Sander heard nothing but the sounds of his brother's helicopter and occasionally Mattias's breathing. Pallan island wasn't a great distance from the mainland, so Sander knew it wouldn't be long at all now until the helicopter reached land and passed close to the family seat.

A few minutes later, Mattias said, "We're about to—oh my *God.*"

Chapter Nine

Sander closed his eyes and drew a deep breath. Mattias was a man rarely moved to extreme displays of emotion, even under intense situations. For his brother to sound so taken aback, so stricken, Sander knew it must be bad. His heart dropped to his stomach. He wondered how he would function if the next words out of Mattias's mouth were, *the whole thing is gone.*

"An enormous chunk of the castle is in ruins. It's obliterated. The blast radius is unbelievable. I see...I see..." Mattias's voice faded, overtaken by the sound of chopper blades.

Sander suffered anguish so great it stole his breath. His heart hammered at a painfully fast clip. And still, words eluded him.

"...vehicles upside down a fourth of a mile from the bailey, fire, pieces of the castle everywhere. It's utter disaster," Mattias shouted.

"Get on the ground and call me back with an update." Sander ended the call and got up from his seat. He approached the cockpit and opened the door. To the pilot and co-pilot, he said, "Fly over Ahtissari castle before you land."

"Yes, your Majesty."

He closed the door and paced through the luxurious interior of the jet. As gilded as his family seat, in white with gold trim, the aircraft looked more like a well appointed apartment than a plane. Several upscale sofas lined two walls, positioned across from each other for ease of conversation. Another section had several regular seats of soft leather. There was a kitchenette and a back bedroom that also served as his office when he wanted to make private phone calls or hold video conferences with diplomats from other countries. Sander focused only on the floor while he walked, compartmentalizing his fear and panic and grief so he could perform his duties as king. He told himself that Chey was tough, as were his children. Maybe she'd been well away from the blast and had survived. Mattias had not said the entire castle was gone, although clearly, an extreme loss of life had occurred. They

125

employed hundreds of staff members and military personnel at the family seat.

"Sander, we're fielding calls from other ambassadors. What do you want us to say? Word is starting to spread about the explosions," one guard said.

"Tell everyone what we know. That right now, there has been an attack. No one has claimed responsibility. Do not mention the Russians whatsoever. We have no proof of anything yet."

"Yes your Majesty."

"It appears three structures were taken out in Somero, Sander. Heavy loss of life," another guard said, voicing the updates aloud.

Sander only nodded once to acknowledge. Not good news. His cell phone rang ten minutes later. He knew it was Mattias, on land, approaching the castle. "Yes."

"It's bad. I estimate a quarter to one third of the castle is nothing but rubble. Dead and wounded everywhere. Fire is burning on three floors. We're looking for a way in," Mattias said. He sounded out of breath. In the background, Sander could hear screams, shouts and other chaos.

"Be careful. We should be landing in

an hour and a half or so."

"I'll call you when...when I find anything," Mattias said, voice grim.

"All right." Sander ended the call. He walked to the back bedroom and closed the door. With methodical precision, he peeled out of his jacket. Throwing it on the bed, he toed out of his shoes and stripped off the slacks. The tie and shirt came next. Catching a glint of metal, he glanced down at his wedding ring. Flashes of his life with Chey went through his mind, such sweet, poignant memories. Some were hot with passion, others of her fiery nature, still more of her with their babies. The sacrifices she'd made for him were great.

Grinding his teeth, he bit back a flood of emotion and went to the small closet. He kept several changes of clothes there for the occasions when he had to fly from one country to another, one meeting to the next, and needed new attire for each. The gear he chose to wear on missions— dark pants with many pockets, a long sleeved black shirt and a vest with more pockets—was also present, and what he pulled off the hangers. He dressed quickly, dragging combat boots from a low shelf. Sliding into a shoulder holster and a weapons belt, he stepped to the other side of the closet and moved aside several hanging shirts. From a hidden safe in the wall, he liberated two handguns and four extra magazines. Loading the holsters and storing the ammunition, he exited the bedroom, ready for anything. They might have been attacked unaware, but he wouldn't arrive on the scene the same way. This was an act of war, as far as he was concerned, and he didn't intend on going into battle unarmed.

* * *

"Coming up on the target," the pilot announced over the speakers.

Sander veered to the window, bracing his hands against the thick sill. As the jet banked, the ruin of his family seat came into view. No matter how he'd prepared himself, how he'd tried to calm his frantic mind, seeing the devastation in person cut him to the core. It looked like the bomb had gone off in the front quadrant of the castle, blowing the entire facade to pieces. Cars, SUVs and several military vehicles that had been in the bailey sat outside the now decimated walls, some on their hoods, others on their sides. The pilot flew at a low enough altitude that Sander could make out the shapes of running bodies and more vehicles—his military—arriving on the long road between the castle and the shoreline.

Part of the castle, the latter half and parts of the east and west wings, were still intact. Intact, but suffering damage. He could see black soot marks on the stone. Sinking into a seat as the jet righted and headed for the private strip, Sander schooled his breathing and told himself that Mattias hadn't called back because he'd not found anything yet. No news was good news, wasn't that the way of it?

A little voice inside insisted that if Mattias *had* found Chey or the children, he would have called by now. Mattias, who knew him almost better than anyone, would call the very moment he had Chey and the kids safe in his presence.

"She's there. She has to be. The kids...the kids are fine," he whispered to himself for the hundredth time.

The jet landed smoothly on the tarmac. Disembarking the second the door was open and the stairs were down, Sander jogged to the waiting Hummer and sat in the front seat rather than the back. His guards needed no prompting to get in. Two more Hummers flanked the one Sander sat in, ready to provide escort to the castle.

"Let's go," Sander told the driver, a man dressed in fatigues who was also armed to the teeth.

The Hummer sped along the road, bypassing other military vehicles that pulled over to give the procession room. Word was out: Sander was en route.

From the back seat, one of the guards brought his phone away from his ear and said, "Sander, Imatra has been attacked. Half a city block is gone."

Sander cursed under his breath. Maybe Konstantine had been right all along. Maybe they *were* under attack by the Russians. What happened to the thirty days notice? Where was Somero's 'warning'? Or Sander's, for that matter? He'd received no 'note' from any Russian commander stating demands.

His attention diverted away from possible invasion to the sight of his family seat. The road leading to the once majestic castle now led to a catastrophic scene straight out of a war movie. The

Hummer had to divert around huge blocks of stone, parts of the wall and facade of the castle, just to reach a stopping point that would allow the men inside room to maneuver once on foot. There was so much damage that Sander didn't at first see any way *in*. Mattias and Leander were here somewhere, though, and he didn't waste a second to get his boots on the ground. Yanking on gloves, he navigated bodies—oh god, *bodies*—and shattered bits of glass, furniture and other innards of the castle.

"Your Majesty!"

Sander paused and turned to Urmas, who, for once, had changed out of his favored suits into clothing more suited to aid with recovery: dark pants, boots, a long sleeved thermal.

"Any news on my wife and my children?" Sander said first.

"We've found four survivors--"

"Only four?"

"...yes. So far, her Highness and the children have not been located. These are the areas inside that are being searched." Urmas handed Sander a hastily hand-drawn 'map'. It was a sketch of the major hallways, wings and rooms. "I drew an X through the rooms that have been thoroughly searched and cleared of victims."

"There are only two marks on here."

"Yes. It's a lot of damage, your Majesty."

"Did you call in extra medical--"

"Some are here and more from the north are on their way," Urmas said, anticipating the question. "Citizens are pouring in from everywhere to help."

"Be sure Kallaster is heavily guarded. Everyone knows that's where I've taken up residence." Sander picked up speed, jogging forward to a point of rubble that he thought he could crest, giving him access to the interior. Many other men, guards and military and those who had been further back in the castle out of blast range crawled over the debris both inside and out, searching for bodies.

Hitting the first pile of rocks at a run, Sander hopped to a higher peak, then another, the map clutched in his gloved hand. He wove his way along the unstable hill of stone, catching glimpses of what used to be his family home. Many walls were gone, some cut in half, others burnt and crumbling. Most items of furniture had been taken apart and flung in several directions, leaving him to straddle the leg of a chair, a piece of couch, or a length of shattered crown molding just to go forward. Some of the debris blocked hallways that were still standing. Men pulled and tugged at the blockades, attempting to gain entrance.

He was reminded of third world countries where bombings were a daily way of life. That was the level of devastation he faced.

"Chey!" he shouted, climbing over a final obstacle to get his feet on somewhat solid ground. "Elias!" To think Chey and his children were somewhere in this madness terrified him.

What should have been an easy search and rescue mission turned out to be anything but. The second he thought he had a way in, rubble shifted or the route proved to be impassable. Many sections had been so shredded that they were not familiar at all, and Sander had to backtrack a few steps to get a bigger view to situate himself. Workers shouted back and forth, using their hands and crowbars to move objects from their path.

It was slow going. Too slow.

Sander penetrated the interior, shouting himself hoarse, and squeezed past a cracked column to enter what used to be a conference room. He used fallen stones to clamber upward, knocking his knee and banging an elbow. Struggling, he got onto an upper floor and had to crawl beneath a blown out door, a tilted table and a sharp piece of glass until he could stand upright. The floor here, this close to the blast radius, felt unstable under his feet. Recognizing a swath of burnt wallpaper, he knew he was on the 'royal' floor, where his room and those of the king and queen once stood. Stepping around a buckled wall, he shouted for Chey, listening in between steps for voices.

Stuffing the map into a pocket, he muscled part of a side table that had wedged into a wall out of the way—and saw a tiny foot beneath a smaller pile of debris a few feet ahead. Soot covered five miniature pink toes.

His chest constricted and he couldn't breathe.

"I need help up here!" he shouted over his shoulder once the initial spasm of shock passed. Sander picked away a piece of drywall, part of a mirror frame, pieces of a headboard and rocks the size of bowling balls. A little leg appeared, the hem of a frilly dress. He uncovered a delicate arm, breath coming harsh and fast, a litany of prayers falling from his lips.

Please, please let her be alive.

Sander moved a wad of mattress and crouched between more debris when he uncovered the child's upper torso. A girl— a redheaded sweetheart he recognized as the daughter of one of the staff. Sander had encouraged his staff to bring their children to an onsite daycare, which had worked out well for everyone, and for which the employees were grateful. Not everyone utilized the service, but many did. Reaching down, Sander felt for a pulse, heart in his throat.

The steady *blip-blip* under his fingertips assured him the girl was still alive.

"I need help up here!" he bellowed again. Sander knew she shouldn't be moved. Not until medical professionals could make sure she was stable.

Scrabbling on the rock pile behind him and puffing breaths preceded the arrival of three men who took over in Sander's wake. He pressed on, confident his men would give the girl the best care.

It took him fifteen minutes just to clear another ten feet of hallway. He shouted for Chey, for his kids, relentless in his search to find them. Sander came upon Gunnar's old bedroom, most of the furniture shoved against a far wall. Natalia's bedroom was in a little better shape, with only one car sized chunk ripped out near the door.

He didn't stop until he'd reached the king's suite, sweat dripping down his forehead.

"Chey!" The suite wasn't as damaged as the other rooms, though mirrors had fallen, the sofas had overturned and one of the chandeliers had lost quite a few crystals that now lay scattered over the floor. Sander ran from room to room in the suite, shouting each of his children's names.

Nothing. No answer. There was not so much damage here that he would have missed their presence.

Leaving the room, he checked the queen's room, and every other suite in the hall. No Chey. No children.

He pushed on, finding another entrance between walls back where there was more damage, intent on searching the middle rooms—or what was left of them—beyond what used to be the foyer.

Sander refused to give up until he

found them, or until someone told him
they were dead.

Chapter Ten

A tickle of smoke ushered Chey into awareness. The scent permeated her senses, bringing forth a fragile cough. When she opened her eyes, she couldn't penetrate the veil of darkness no matter how many times she blinked. Confused and disoriented, she tried to remember what happened. How she'd come to be flat on her back, dazed and dizzy, with something heavy pinning her body to the floor.

"Sander?" she wheezed, struggling against the seemingly immovable object—the arm of a couch, perhaps, if the brocade against her fingertips was any indication—that she attempted to push off her hips.

A pathetic whimper sounded from somewhere to her right.

"Hello?" She coughed again, pushing harder, the whimper triggering her motherly instincts. Another whimper sent spikes of fear down her spine. Suddenly desperate to free herself, sure that her children were in danger or hurt, she used a foot to brace against the inverted sofa.

"Baby? Erick?" Memory returned between one heartbeat and the next. They'd been playing a board game in one of the informal living rooms on the second floor when—something had happened. All she remembered was a force striking her from behind and then nothingness.

"Elias! Emily!" She shouted, the sound contained within the smothering confines of the sofa. Chey recognized pain in her side, in her wrist and on her head, but that didn't stop her from shoving against the heavy couch. It must have been braced on another piece of debris, relieving most—but not all—of the crushing weight.

"Erick!" she shouted again. Another whimper. Chey scooted her hand under the edge of the tilted sofa, feeling around for something. Anything. She made contact with a little arm.

"Erick!" With a surge of adrenaline, she dragged her legs up, almost a tuck-and-roll position, pain screaming along her insides. She scraped skin off her shin and didn't care. Gathering her feet, she started to kick out at the sofa, then realized that if she succeeded in bouncing it off her body, she might inadvertently crush one of her children. Using her feet and her hands, she caught the edge of the sofa and maneuvered it up enough to scoot out from beneath. She bumped into several other objects she couldn't identify. It was difficult to see, as well, the once bright room now doused in gloom.

Half under a piece of coffee table, she spied her baby, Erick, flat on his back, face covered in soot. He whimpered again.

Chey shoved at a cushion, cut her hand on a sliver of glass, and pulled herself across the floor to her youngest child. "Erick, baby. Open your eyes and look at mommy." She glanced at the debris field around them, then shouted into the mess of furniture and blown out walls. "Emily! Elias!"

Dear God. Her children were in here somewhere. There must have been an explosion. Gas line—something. She didn't know what. If it would have been an earthquake, she would remember more before the sudden blast. Then she remembered the situation with Imatra and the supposed attacking Russians. Could this have been the work of someone making a point? Sander had thought Konstantine's words treaded too close to a promise of action against Latvala.

"Erick?" Chey pushed another piece of cushion off Erick's shoulder and breathed a small sigh of relief when he let out a yowl and rolled toward her, blinking soot out of his eyes. She gathered him close, looking for other injuries. He seemed to be moving all his limbs without any trouble. He cried into her chest and held on with both arms.

"Emily! Elias!" Chey coughed and struggled to free herself and Erick from the rest of the debris. That she couldn't hear anything from her other two children sent cold spikes of fear down her spine. *Please, please let them be all right.*

Fearing another, bigger blast, she kicked at a ruined end table and moved against the field of wrecked paintings, bits of shattered wall and the tangle of a lamp cord, desperate for a glimpse of Emily and Elias. Disoriented, she called out again, clutching Erick against her body. Thin swirls of smoke made it difficult to see, though she didn't think anything in the room was on fire.

Erick whimpered, then let out another squall.

In that moment, when she realized how traumatized her child was, and that her other two were not accounted for, fury seized her and made it hard to think. The anger blazed hot for that single moment before terror took hold again.

"Emily! Elias! Can you hear me? Make some noise for me." She crawled two feet on her knees and it felt like two miles. It was like trying to wade into the ocean while enormous waves were crashing against her legs. There was just so much wreckage.

Beyond an overturned chair, she glimpsed a shred of pink beneath a mound of rubble. Emily had been wearing a pink tee shirt before the explosion. She pushed a shattered piece of wood aside, calling out to her daughter, agonized at the thought of Emily beneath the pile. Reaching the scrap of pink, she settled Erick on her hip to better have use of her other hand. She angled several boards out of the way, the drape of a tapestry and several sections of molding. The furniture they had been sitting on when the blast ripped through the room had provided a *little* protection, forcing some of the debris into a tee-pee type position over Emily, who came into view when

Chey cleared out another damaged painting.

"Emily!" The little girl who so resembled her mother groaned and fluttered her lashes, then coughed. Chey moved closer, looking for wounds or broken bones, and felt a rush of panic when she spied blood on Emily's forehead. Emily pealed out a terrified noise that reduced to a cough.

"I need help in here! Hello?" Chey called out as loud as she could.

She didn't know if anyone else was still alive to come to their aid.

* * *

Sander found five dead bodies in his search. Every pale or bloody glimpse of skin had taken a year off his life. No matter what else happened, people he considered family and friends, not just employees, had perished. He also found two survivors, none of which were Chey or his children. Sander handed the survivors off to several arriving medics and returned to his search.

Clearing three half damaged rooms, he moved closer to a more decimated area, forced to pitch pieces of debris aside to make any progress. He had scraped knuckles and a banged up knee, but disregarded the minor injuries while he sought more victims—and his family. His chest was tight with suppressed panic.

"Chey!" He cupped his hands around his mouth, calling forward in hopes to hear *something.* Anything. He called for his kids, too, and heard an echo from somewhere beyond the next damaged room.

Mattias's voice.

Making it through what used to be a doorway, Sander stood inside one of the informal living areas, now three-quarters decimated with the far wall blown out, exposing the opposite hallway in another wing. He saw Mattias sifting through the rubble.

"Thought I heard something in here," he shouted.

"Hello? Sander?"

Sander's heart stuttered when he heard Chey's voice. Distant, faint, coming somewhere beyond a pile of broken furniture and debris from a partially collapsed ceiling. "Chey!"

He pushed through, careful where he stepped and where he tossed damaged pieces of debris. If Chey was here, his kids were likely not far away.

"She's on the other side," Mattias shouted.

"I hear her!" he shouted back.

"I can't find Elias! We need medical attention up here for Emily and Erick."

Sander quelled a rush of nausea to hear Chey hadn't found Elias. He worried about the damage to his other two children while he made progress through the room, bellowing for the medics. He came upon Chey, kneeling on the ground, holding Erick to one side of her body while bracing several sections of wood and plaster above a moaning Emily. Soot streaked, dark hair wild around her head, Chey looked to be in good shape despite a few scrapes and a trickle of blood below an earlobe. The relief he experienced was brief.

In minutes he'd cleared enough of the debris so that Emily could sit up and crawl to Chey. She had a cut on her head, several bruises on her cheek and one on her arm, but didn't seem to be suffering any broken bones. Internal damage, he couldn't say. He expended a single moment to kiss the three of them on their heads before he shouted for Elias.

"Over here!" Mattias called.

Sander twisted to look where Mattias was helping Elias out from under an overturned coffee table. He saw that Mattias had shoved aside a small settee to get to his nephew.

"Elias!" Sander kicked remnants of a vase to the side. Elias coughed, appearing disoriented as if he'd just come to, then threw his arms around Mattias's neck.

"Dad," Elias murmured, holding tight while Mattias navigated his way to meet Sander in the middle. Sander exchanged a look with Mattias before taking his son in his arms.

"Dad, I can't breathe," Elias complained with a cough.

"I know, I'm sorry." Sander hugged his eldest son tight, then loosened his hold. He didn't want to exacerbate any internal damage his child might have suffered.

"Chey and the kids all right?" Mattias asked, as the men made their way back to her.

"I think so. They all need to go to the hospital to be checked out." No one was missing arms or legs or appeared to be experiencing extreme amounts of pain. Sander sent up a silent prayer of thanks.

Reaching Chey, who had both kids in her arms and was pushing to stand,

Sander used one arm to hug her, Erick and Emily to his side. He needed a minute to feel their breath, hear their soft noises, feel the warmth of their skin. To reassure himself this was real, that they were *alive*.

"I'm so glad you're all right," Sander murmured to the lot of them. It was a wild understatement. "Let's get you out of here. We'll take the hallway, it's clearer at the back."

Sander guided his family out of the mess, meeting up with medics who had finally made their way to this floor.

"I want radio silence when you transfer them to the hospital," Sander said to the emergency team. They were his men, from his country, foretold by the clothing that differentiated them from foreign medical teams beginning to arrive on the scene. "Under no circumstances do I want it announced over any radio—or phone for that matter—where my wife and kids are going. Use the private entrance at the hospital and take extra security with you."

"Wait, Sander. You're not coming?" Chey asked, turning her soot streaked face his way.

Sander pressed a careful kiss to her

mouth, holding Elias snug against him, one hand cradling Emily's head. He said, "I can't. I have to search for survivors, Chey. There are a lot of people still missing. Tell security to send a coded message to my men here if there's anything life threatening for any of you and I'll come right away."

"I understand. Be careful. I don't like the thought that this might not be over."

"Exactly. I'll be careful." Sander kissed each one of his children and hugged them one more time, hating to be parted from them after such a short reconciliation.

He sent them with the medics and several security that had arrived to escort the queen and his heirs to a waiting chopper.

Sander glanced at Mattias. He read the same relief in his brother's eyes, yet also concern that the attacks might not be over. "I was told Imatra suffered an attack as well. Heard anything about it?"

Mattias looked surprised, then frowned. "Nothing. Do you think it could be the Russians, like Konstantine said?"

"I don't know. I just don't know. Let's look for survivors and we'll see what's going on after that. The military is on high alert. Hopefully they'll radio in with an update soon." Sander feared another attack might happen in the big city of Kalev or that troops would swarm the borders before Latvala was ready.

As he returned to the search with Mattias, Sander recalled Konstantine's last words at Kallaster castle: *Before this week is through, you will be groveling to take me up on my offer, mark my words.*

Chapter Eleven

The search and rescue—and recovery
—lasted into dawn of the following day.
Eighty-three people had perished in the
attack on Ahtissari castle, which by now
had made headlines world wide. Sander
mourned every loss, from security to
kitchen staff to several high ranking
advisors. Most of the men and women
working side by side with the king and
the princes performed their tasks in
silence, their faces bearing proof of their
internal grief. Many had been friends with
the deceased.

Sander received updates from Urmas
on Chey and the children's status. A few
stitches, bruised ribs, scrapes, and a
couple of sprains was the extent of the
damage. The physical damage.
Psychologically, no one could say.
Children overall tended to be very
resilient in the face of tragedy, but Sander
suffered for them nevertheless. He hated
to think it would scar his kids for the rest

of their lives. They were alive, however, and for that he was eternally thankful.

Standing near a military vehicle in the bailey, Sander tipped up a cold bottle of water and drained half in one go. His clothes were filthy, with rips and tears from climbing through the debris field. Mattias, Gunnar and Leander looked the same. They had tirelessly sought survivors through the night, taking few breaks in between. Coming in bursts from news reports, Sander had learned that at least four hundred people had died in Somero, and another hundred and fifty in Imatra. Konstantine's capital had been hit, with two civil buildings the target of a bombing.

Sander didn't know what to make of it. Three countries, three separate attacks, all before the 'due date' on the Russian note. There had been no mention of bombings—then again, the note hadn't specified *what* might happen should Imatra neglect to comply. That the Russians had bombed Latvala and Somero made little sense to Sander, considering neither had received any kind of formal letter, as Konstantine had, nor any forewarning of an attack.

Something was wrong. Very wrong.

Via code, through an intermediary in his army, Sander sent a message to the security detail to move Chey and the kids to a safe house in Kalev. A safe house with a large bunker underground that should—*should*—protect them if more bombs fell.

In the hours following, Sander learned that the explosion had come from a suitcase left on the premises of Ahtissari castle. Someone had smuggled it inside and detonated from a remote location. With as many people that came and went, it wouldn't be easy to track down the perpetrator. The log of visitors had gone up in the blast, making the task harder.

Urmas informed him Somero and Imatra had both suffered the same kind of attack, with a bomb left behind in a bag or a briefcase. The coordinated assault had been planned—but by who?

Catching up with Mattias and Leander a while after that, Sander ran a hand through his disheveled hair, staring up at what used to be the family seat. He felt strangely violated, as if something once precious had been stripped away. Sander had not had a wonderfully happy childhood, at least not where his father was concerned, but he'd grown up here with his brothers and that meant more to him than anything. The history behind the castle meant something as well. He avoided the place, yes, but he wouldn't have ever dreamed of bringing the structure to ruin. A dominant part of his children's legacy was now nothing more than a scene of destruction. They could rebuild, of course, and probably should. That didn't detract from the knowledge that the structure itself had suffered a significant amount of damage and that the integrity of the castle might now be in jeopardy. There was something to be said for the memories locked within these walls, walls that would never be the same again. Many important portraits of his ancestors had been spared—some had not. If he had ever thought someone would take such a drastic measure against him, he would have had each and every one committed to a safer haven.

"So far, there have been no more reports of attacks elsewhere in the country," Mattias said, brushing chalky dust from his pants. His clothes were as ruined as Sander's. Leander, too, sported a few tears in his dusty pants and soot marks on his hands and forearms.

"Or Imatra and Somero, for that

matter. I'd like to get my hands on whoever the mastermind is," Leander said with a shake of his head. He stared at the decimated castle with an expression of disgust and dismay and subtle flickers of anger.

Sander understood the anger. At times, he'd been so furious it was hard to continue the search. He'd wanted to switch to the perpetrator, focus all his energy on bringing the entity responsible to justice.

He still couldn't believe any of it had happened. A direct strike in the heart of Latvala was a devastating blow. His family had nearly lost their lives. Although Latvala had not escaped its own mayhem and strife, they had also never experienced a bombing of this magnitude. All these years, he'd struggled and fought to bring the country back from his brother's meddling, and now there was some new adversary to worry about. Other countries and nations the world over were experiencing serious issues of terrorism and turmoil, and he had counted himself lucky not to be involved in it. He did not want Latvala to become embroiled in territory disputes which might send his country to war for years.

"Yes, I'm with you, Leander. I'd like ten minutes alone with the person who orchestrated all this. I'm sure Thane feels the same," Sander said.

"Konstantine?" Mattias asked.

"I can't tell if you're asking whether I'd like to speak to him, or whether I think he's behind it," Sander said. "The latter doesn't seem likely though. Not with an attack on his own soil."

"Your Majesty, you need to see this." Urmas strode toward the men with an electronic device in hand.

Sander peered down at the screen as Mattias and Leander crowded closer to see as well. Urmas turned the sound up as a news video began to play. Konstantine stood before twenty microphones positioned on a podium, his face a mask of stark concern and concentration.

Konstantine looked at the mass of gathered reporters and said, "As you all know, a devastating explosion rocked Imatra yesterday, killing more than a hundred and fifty people. Innocents, citizens who didn't deserve to die. Last week, I received a threat from a Russian commander to allow Imatra to be brought into Russia's fold, a threat I took seriously. In my quest to remain independent of the Russian hegemony, I sought the aid of King Sander Ahtissari of Latvala."

Sander muttered a few colorful curses and said, "Here it comes."

Konstantine, reading from a paper in his hands, continued after whispers from reporters quieted down. "I approached the king as a desperate measure, asking for help after the Russians attacked and killed several of my troops near the border. King Ahtissari flatly declined. In retrospect, I can understand that he may not have had all the information he needed at the time. But I'm asking now, pleading with King Sander to reconsider the terms I asked for upon my visit."

Sander tuned out when Konstantine began listing the buildings and amount of damage, and started taking questions from the press.

"Well, we know what that was all about," Leander said.

"A public knock on me, that's what," Sander added, snorting in disgust. He rubbed his face with his hands. "Konstantine should know better than to address something so crucial in front of the media."

"They'll hound you now, even more than before," Mattias said. "They'll want to know what the terms are. Konstantine isn't stupid enough to say *that* on live television."

Sander shot his brother a doubtful look. "He's broken protocol. There are just *some* things that should never make it to the media. I suppose he feels pressured, however."

"You're not thinking of joining Latvala with Imatra, are you?" Leander asked, sending Sander a concerned look.

"Of course not. We all need to secure our own borders. At the very least, I'll have my armies fight alongside Thane's and maybe Imatra, if it comes to that. But I won't consider giving up our sovereignty. The Russians or whoever it was that bombed us will have to kill me first." Sander wasn't about to be bullied or coerced despite the dire circumstances.

Urmas, who had been listening intently, said, "You'll get your chance sooner than later to question Konstantine. This was recorded hours ago and he has already sent a request for a meeting later today."

"That bastard really is going to press

157

for unification," Leander said in disbelief.

"He's running scared," Mattias replied. "Konstantine isn't cut out to be king. He's got grandiose ambitions that are not in the least feasible or reasonable and, in my opinion from the rumors I've heard, is running Imatra by the seat of his pants. Someone comes knocking on his door and bam, he's fleeing to the neighbor for help —and thinks Sander is stupid enough to hand over the kingdom simply because a disaster has struck. He's delusional."

"Tell Konstantine my answer is still--" Sander paused. He considered his options while Mattias, Leander and Urmas waited on his reply. "No, tell him I want the meeting. Later, in Kalev. Arrange it for the penthouse in the hotel but don't tell him or his security where they're going until they get there. If he or his guards balk, then send them home. I'm not giving out my whereabouts freely right now."

"What have you got up your sleeve, old man?" Leander said, squinting curiously at Sander.

"I'm going to find out exactly how much he knows, and whether he's withholding information. My inner alarm bells are still going off, and it doesn't all have to do with the catastrophe I'm

158

staring at." Sander couldn't explain his suspicions or the lingering feeling that Konstantine knew more than he let on.

"Well. You *did* wonder if he was bluffing about the photos. Maybe you're onto something. I don't know if that means he knew an attack was imminent and meant to strong-arm or scare you into merging countries, or if he actually had a hand in the planning—then got surprised with an attack on his own country," Leander said.

"We can't rule out anything. All of us here are well aware of how much propaganda and misinformation gets spread between leaders, advisors, ambassadors and the media in general. Everyone's got a different story to tell, and most of the time, there's a lot more going on behind the scenes than people ever hear," Sander added.

"I'll arrange it," Urmas said, and walked briskly away.

"Maybe you shouldn't meet up with Konstantine alone," Leander said once Urmas was out of earshot.

"I'll be careful. I doubt he'd do something brazen, like bring a weapon into the meeting. The hotel has its own security as well and should detect anything on him when he enters," Sander said.

"Good. Let us know what he says. You'll have to talk to the press sooner than later. Or do you want me to take care of it?" Mattias asked.

"Actually, yes. Would you? I'll prepare the statement and you can read it in my stead. I want to see Chey and the kids before I hit the meeting with Konstantine, so I'll write it sometime between now and then." Sander let out a slow breath. He needed to calm his mind to write something coherent and cohesive.

"All right. We'll see you later. Should I tell the press that you'll make a statement tomorrow?" Mattias asked. "I can fill in today, but I think the people will want to see you in person to make sure you weren't a casualty of the blast. As well as other heads of state. I'm sure everyone is on pins and needles, wondering if you're really alive."

Sander snorted. "I'm sure the vultures are circling even though they know that you'll take the throne in the intermediate time until Elias is old enough to accept the responsibility. Yes, I'll make an appearance tomorrow."

After departing his brother and

Leander's presence, Sander allowed several guards to drive him to the helipad. When they were airborne, he looked down over the remains of Ahtissari castle with a heavy heart, then turned his mind to his wife and children.

A bright spot in an otherwise dismal day.

* * *

Chey, torn between duties as queen and mother to her children, gave each equal measure of her time. Once she was sure the kids were calm and comfortable, she ushered them into a small but serviceable shower in Sander's office, a spare room with only one desk, three chairs and huge maps tacked to the walls. There was a bunk bed, a small niche for clothes and a modest bathroom. Nothing kingly, yet it allowed him a secure place to make calls and plan missions.

She washed what was left of the grime and dust off their bodies and out of their hair, then changed them into clothes provided by guards who had made a secretive trip to Kallaster. The less people who knew where Chey and the kids were, the better. Chey had taken her turn under the hot spray, wincing once or twice at the sting against a particular bruise or abrasion on her skin. Preferring to wear regular clothes to sleep, she tossed and turned, unable to shut her mind down enough to get any real rest. The children woke several times with gasps or quiet cries, which Chey soothed before they fell back to sleep.

In the morning, weary but determined to get things done, Chey dressed in a sensible outfit of dark wool slacks and a long sleeved sweater the color of wine, adding a pair of lace up shoes with good tread.

She busied the kids with activities such as drawing and reading. Trusting their safety with two guards, Chey walked the maze of tunnels, getting to know the layout. Solid stone surrounded her on every side, which was both mildly disconcerting and comforting at the same time. There were only a few ways in or out of the bunker and security had informed her of its safe haven status. Only a select number of employees even knew of its existence. It was used in extreme circumstances when Sander needed to totally disappear from the public eye.

She met with the man in charge, Mister Olsen, to go over escape plans should there be a breach of the bunker. Chey hadn't wanted to discuss it in front of the kids, worried they might fret about their safety and not find any peace. Their moods were tenuous in the wake of the explosion anyway, swinging from staunch to sobbing in a heartbeat.

Once she had examined all the routes in and out—mostly out—Chey got on a secure line to Kallaster castle. She informed her assistant of all the usual tasks that needed doing, and that she herself wouldn't be giving any interviews with media. Chey told her assistant to direct all inquiries and questions to Urmas, who would be handling the fallout. She spent an hour dealing with instructions to certain charities she ran, keeping the volunteers up to date while she was effectively out of circulation. Working with the charities had become one of her favorite passions besides her kids, her husband and photography. She adored helping all those people, many of them children. Sander often joined her, which made the activity all the sweeter. Both for her and for the charity.

On her way back to the kids some time

later, Chey checked her cell phone for messages. She hadn't been able to use the phone underground and discovered she still didn't have a signal. The landlines were the only way to get communications in or out. Computers, maybe, but she didn't have one here.

Rounding a corner, she bumped into a rock hard body.

"Oh, pardon—Sander!" Chey glanced up after making contact with his chest. She threw her arms around his neck, phone in one hand. "I was just looking to see if you left me a message."

Sander caught her around the waist and turned a slow circle, lifting her feet off the floor. "Reception is crap down here," he said, voice a quiet rumble.

Leaning her head back, she sought his eyes. It never failed to thrill her how easily he made it seem to hold her aloft. Today, the thrill was tempered by the somber realization of loss. "How did it go? I heard eighty-three people died."

"A lot of deaths, yes. Konstantine has asked to meet with me here in a little while, but I wanted to stop by and see you and the kids. I just left their room."

"I'm glad you got to see them. They've been anxious," she admitted.

164

"I could tell. Em cried for five minutes when I was trying to leave. They all look so fragile, even Elias." Sander exhaled a slow breath.

"I know. They're holding on, though I'm really worried they'll have nightmares or, at the very least, restless sleep again. To be honest, I don't think I'll sleep much better tonight than I did last night." Chey smoothed her fingers from Sander's temple to the back of his head. He looked rough, clothes dirty, face smudged with soot. She knew he'd been searching throughout the night.

"That really pisses me off. Don't get me wrong, I'm so thankful you're all alive, but knowing you and the kids might suffer emotionally infuriates me."

"I know. There's nothing we can do except try to make the kids feel secure from now on and make sure they're in constant contact with us." Chey paused, then said, "What do you think Konstantine will say?"

"The same thing he said before, with more fervency behind it." Sander's eyes shuttered, shielding some of what he was thinking.

Chey caught a glimmer of caution in Sander's expression before he closed it off.

"So you think he'll still push for a merger? What happens if it *is* the Russians and they attack all three countries again? Will you be forced to join up with Imatra and Somero to save Latvala?"

"We'll fight *alongside,* as in we would all fight to save our sovereignty, but I won't ever consider a full on merger. Latvala won't be 'absorbed' into Imatra, period. We'll go to war, and hopefully our allies will step in to give us aid. Konstantine is grasping, he's not thinking everything through. He's only had the throne a year and from what I've heard, he's driving Imatra into the ground."

"Could that be why Russia decided to strike? Because they sensed weakness?" Chey asked. Sometimes, the extreme politics and strategizing went far beyond her mien. But certain questions presented themselves and she preferred to have answers so she better understood Sander's point of view.

"Remember, we have no solid proof yet that it was Russia--"

"What kind of proof will you need? For their army to march across the border?" Chey wasn't being facetious; she genuinely wanted to know how Latvala's military would figure out who had precipitated the attack.

"That would be one way," he said with a quirk of his lips. "Or we find some identifying marker left at the scene, or they take responsibility in public."

"Didn't they do that with the letter?"

"It's damning, I'll say that much," Sander admitted. "But there's still a question in my mind. Those photos I saw first, of the supposed Russian attack, just don't sit right with me. I could be wrong—I've been wrong before. I need more proof to retaliate and bomb Russia, who could literally blow Latvala, Somero and Imatra right off the map in a heartbeat. If it *wasn't* them, and we lob bombs across the border, then they're well within their rights to strike back and judiciously so. I won't risk all those lives on poor intel and 'maybes'."

Chey pulled one arm down to tuck her phone into her pocket, so that she had both arms free to slide around his neck. "I didn't think of it that way. I guess it just seems, from my point of view, very hard to find out who is to blame."

"One thing you have to remember is that everyone has an agenda. Not all

167

agendas are violent or motivated by greed, but many are. Just because something *seems* one way, doesn't necessarily mean that's the truth. Trying to suss out the reality from illusion can be tricky, because ultimately, I'm responsible for whatever lives are lost in a confrontation that *I* precipitate. If I have proof of an attack and an invasion, then of course we send people in. Right now, there are too many questions." He smoothed his hand up and down her spine, holding her body to his effortlessly.

"I see." Chey did, and didn't. The semantics of war were difficult for her to follow, considering she came at it from a different point of view than Sander. "How long do you think me and the kids will have to stay here? I'd like to go back to Kallaster if you think it's safe."

"I don't. Right now, this is one of a few places I think you're all secure. Give me a few days to figure this out." He bent to press a warm, lingering kiss against her lips.

Chey encouraged the kiss, relishing the contact. She didn't know when she would see him again. "That's fine. I'll keep the kids busy while they heal."

"I'll get you out of here as soon as I

can, promise." Sander loosened his hold, allowing her feet to touch the ground. Just as he released her, the sound of jogging footsteps in the corridor behind him brought Sander's attention around.

Chey glanced past Sander's shoulder, hands falling away from his arms. One of the guards approached at a quick clip, uniform buttons gleaming in the low lit passageway.

"What is it?" Sander asked the guard even before he arrived.

"Your Majesty, Prince Mattias called on the landline. He needs you back at the family seat immediately," the guard said. He bowed his head to Chey in deference, then looked back at Sander.

"Another attack?" Sander's body tensed.

Chey laid a hand on his arm and held her breath, a tingle of fear creeping across her scalp.

"No, but Mattias said it's urgent. He wouldn't specify what the problem is, only that you need to go back before your meeting with Konstantine."

"That's in less than two hours. It's going to be cutting it close." Sander kissed Chey once more, hard and fast. "I'll call you when I know more."

"Okay. Please be careful." Chey hesitated to let him go. She worried another attack was imminent and that this time, Sander would be at ground zero when it happened.

"I will. Be prepared to move at a moments notice, just in case," he said, then turned away with the guard.

Chey watched the men kick into a jog, disappearing down the passageway around a corner. She exhaled a slow breath and hoped that whatever news Mattias had, it would bring about the end of the terror.

Chapter Twelve

Sander stepped into the nerve center of the underground bunker, a rather plain chamber of stone with several televisions on the wall and a handful of desks manned by security who kept constant watch on the grounds above the bunker via a video feed. He went straight to a handset that another guard handed over.

"Mattias is still on the line."

"Thanks. What's going on?" Sander said into the phone, glancing at the monitors on the wall. The outside streets of Kalev were displayed from different angles around the safe house, which was a fairly impenetrable structure in itself. Made of the same stone as the bunker, the safe house stood on its own plot of land smack in the middle of the city, with underground tunnels providing protection and escape routes should the need arise.

"I need you back here immediately," Mattias said. "I can't say why over the line."

"On a scale of urgency, where are we? I've got the meeting with Konstantine I need to prepare for. The guard said it was important." Sander wanted to hear it from Mattias's mouth, however.

"On a one to ten, we're at an eight."

"Do I need to send Chey and the kids away?" Sander knew Mattias was aware of where Chey and the children were staying, but Sander chose to be vague in case someone was listening in.

"I don't know yet. Keep her on alert though."

Sander didn't like the sound of that. It made him think there was another attack on the horizon. What the hell was going on here?

"I'm on my way." Sander hung up. "I want someone in constant contact with the queen and the children. At the slightest provocation, or on a call from me or Mattias, you get them out of the country, is that understood?" He wasn't taking any more chances with his family. They were easy targets for someone who wanted to strike at the heart of his empire.

"Your Majesty," the guards said, acknowledging the order.

"Where should we take them?" one

man asked.

There were several places Sander could think of. He decided to lean on an old friend in this instance, someone with as much power as he himself had, someone who could provide a safe haven far from Latvala's shores until the situation blew over.

"Afshar. Take them to the Emir. I'll make a call on my way back to Ahtissari castle." Sander left the room. Afshar, a small but vibrant country in the mid-eastern bloc, was home to one of Sander's good friends. A man named Ahsan, who Sander trusted with his life. And that of his family. Ahsan would make sure nothing happened to Chey or the kids. Ahsan had armies of his own to protect his shores.

From the nerve center, Sander made a brief stop to shower and change, again choosing dark clothing better suited for situations where he might be required to fight or go on the run. He didn't know what to expect from Mattias's call, so he prepared in advance for battle. Arming himself from a small cache in the closet, he met up with his guards and exited the building via a separate, secret tunnel that opened up onto another part of the street away from the safe house.

Climbing into a black Hummer waiting at the curb, Sander turned his mind away from his family to the urgent matter awaiting back at the ruined castle.

He feared Mattias was about to tell him there were foreign troops on the border, ready to invade.

* * *

En route to Ahtissari castle, Sander made good on his promise. He contacted Ahsan and arranged a safe haven for his family should it come to that. Ahsan offered his help in the interim, whether physically, financially or militarily. Sander asked Ahsan to be on standby and the Emir, close friends with Sander for years, easily agreed. Sander answered several other select messages left on his private phone from other close allies, putting each on stand by status as well. If, God forbid, Latvala was about to be invaded, he would need all the help he could get.

On the helipad after the chopper landed, Sander crossed to a waiting Hummer. The sun streamed down through a scuttling layer of clouds, refracting off the gleaming black paint of the vehicle. The landscape surrounding the castle looked the same as it ever had, pretty and lush and still green this late in the season, which made the destruction of the castle an uglier blight on the land. On the drive from the helipad, down a long road circumventing the family seat, Sander took note of the extensive military presence surrounding the property. Soldiers with weapons in their hands surveyed the flat lands and the distant treeline, on the alert for trespassers—or enemies.

Another Hummer sat cockeyed in the road well before the now damaged gate, forcing Sander's vehicle to slow to a stop. Sander easily recognized Mattias standing in the road alongside another stranger, with troops making a loose circle of protection around the prince.

Sander disembarked and walked the short distance to his brother. On the way, he sized up the stranger. Short brown hair, pug nose, black rimmed eyeglasses, civilian clothing. He wore brown pants paired with a plain white button down and suede saddleback shoes. Sander couldn't place him. He wasn't an advisor, a councilman or anyone of that stature.

In fact, the closer Sander got, the more young the man seemed. Early to middle twenties.

"Sander, thanks for coming so quickly," Mattias said by way of greeting.

"What's the urgency?" Sander asked Mattias, though his gaze was on the stranger.

"This is Mikel Allanson. He first called a generic number to reach a secretary for the council, who turned him over to Urmas, who then contacted me. He has been telling me a most interesting story that you need to hear," Mattias said.

Mikel shuffled his feet and looked from Mattias to Sander. He appeared slightly nervous, one hand shooting out as if for a handshake before retracting. Mikel seemed uncertain of the protocol for meeting the king.

Sander, in no mood to pander to anyone, took a deep breath for patience and caught Mikel's hand during one of the in-out-in-out advances to shake. He wouldn't stand on ceremony when the man clearly had something interesting to divulge.

"Mikel."

"Your Majesty," Mikel said. His accent matched that of Konstantine.

Sander released the man's sweaty hand, resisting the urge to smear his own palm on his thigh to remove the dampness. He wasn't sure what to think of the Imatra accent. "What information have you given Mattias?" Sander asked, getting right to the point.

Mikel glanced from the king to the prince, then back again. He adjusted his eyeglasses twice, a nervous habit, then cleared his throat.

Mattias interrupted to quietly say, "Tell him like you told me. It'll be all right."

Mikel nodded, then dove into his story. "I could not stay silent after I saw the footage of the attack on your castle. Several weeks ago—well. I should start by saying that I work in King Konstantine's inner circle. I'm his—I *was*—his secondary personal assistant. The assistant to his assistant, yes?" Mikel looked worriedly at Mattias, who inclined his head in a *go on* fashion.

"I follow," Sander said, in hopes of putting the man at ease.

"Several weeks ago, I overheard Konstantine discussing one of the letters he received from the Russians. He was talking to one of his advisors. Konstantine was...how to say it. *Very* upset about the idea of Imatra being absorbed into Russia. He went on and on to the advisor, stating that he knew his army wasn't big enough to fight back and win. That he needed more men. That it was a do or die situation and that Imatra had to do whatever it took to secure its safety. A few days after that, I was called into a private meeting where plans were laid out for the first 'attack' on the border. We staged the whole thing. I was in charge of planning the layout of the bodies and making sure it looked like a battle had taken place."

Sander listened as the story unfolded, biding his time when certain questions popped up along the way. His jaw tightened when Mikel admitted that the first attack had been staged, just as Sander had thought. His instinct that something had been wrong with the entire set up had proven true.

"What about the bodies, though?" he asked. "They looked like dead people to me. Or did you hire professional make up artists?"

"No, no, they were dead people. Real dead people. We used fresh bodies from the morgue and...and..." Mikel looked at the ground.

"And put bullets in them, or hacked out chunks, or laid them atop grenades and after detonation, put the pieces together again in your staged area," Sander said. The thought made him sick.

"Yes. Yes. Exactly. We did the same for the second attack. Konstantine paid certain members of the military off to act out the scene and to keep their mouths shut." Mikel glanced from Mattias to Sander.

"And he did so because his ultimate plan was to come to me with his ridiculous idea to merge countries. So that he could increase his army twofold, and perhaps threefold if we, together, tried to get Somero on board. And if Konstantine staged those scenes, then he's probably the one responsible for the attacks on Thane and I. He arranged—*planned*—for those bombs to go off. He's massacred hundreds and hundreds of people." Sander narrowed his eyes. "Did you have anything to do with planning that, too?"

"No, no! I swear, I never heard anyone breathe a word about the bombs. I didn't hear the regular assistant, my direct boss, ever say anything about it. I also didn't see or hear him planning anything, so I don't know how Konstantine arranged it. But he must have, which is why I'm here. I cannot believe he took it to that extreme and I can't condone the killing of hundreds and hundreds of people. I won't be a part of it any longer." Mikel rubbed his hands together, a traditional gesture of anxiety.

"Konstantine would have kept something like that as close to the vest as possible," Sander said of the bombings. "Although honestly, considering you helped stage the other attacks, I don't see why he wouldn't have engaged your aid again. You already knew what was going on."

"I never heard *anyone* talking about the bombings. Not even whispers or rumors. That part is a bit confusing for me because I am in and out of the king's office all day long. I just think that Konstantine planned it with his military advisors and kept everyone else in the dark so that it didn't leak out. What about the bomb on his own country, however? Why would he hit his own people? I have friends in that area," Mikel said.

"Konstantine isn't known in elite circles for the strength of his mind,"

Mattias said. "He could very well have struck his own city to increase sympathy for Imatra, a way to try and coerce Latvala and Somero to join."

"You said 'was' in reference to being his second assistant," Sander said to Mikel. "Does that mean you quit?"

"I did. I cited a family emergency and walked out. Then I made my way here to tell you what I know in exchange for amnesty. Konstantine will kill me if I return for divulging state secrets," Mikel said.

"And how do I know that you're not actually a spy, sent here to learn as much as you can learn? Perhaps Konstantine wants an inside man, and what better way than to send someone like you." Sander had been through too much, lived too long in this world, to instantly put his trust in someone. He understood how the governments of the world worked, knew that there were plants and spies in all regimes.

Mikel's eyes widened and he held his hands up in a 'stop' gesture. "What? No, never! I am no spy! I swear on my grandfather's grave. I came here only to tell the truth about Konstantine so that no one else will die."

"You may stay for now, but you're under temporary watch until I get more information. The guards will see to you. If you've nothing to hide, we'll know it soon enough." Sander ended the conversation by having two guards escort Mikel to a waiting SUV. From there, the assistant to Konstantine would be cared for while Sander sought more answers.

"I hadn't thought about him possibly being a spy," Mattias said when he and Sander were alone.

"At this point, I don't think we can trust anyone outside our inner circle. It would be a good way to get someone inside Latvala to report troop movements and everything else." Sander muttered a curse, then added, "I knew something was up with those photos."

"Indeed, your instincts are right on. What are you going to say to Konstantine?" Mattias asked.

Sander glanced at his watch. He only had a few minutes to spare before returning to Kalev to meet Konstantine. "In light of these revelations, it'll be all I can do not to punch him in the mouth and drag him off to a holding cell."

"I agree. Do you want me to come with you?"

"No. Stay here and oversee this. Find out what you can about this Mikel person. I want to know if he's really an assistant to Konstantine, who his family is, and whatever else you can find out."

"I'll do it. Be careful. There's no telling if Konstantine has arranged any other 'surprises' along the way."

Sander clapped Mattias on the shoulder. "You be careful, too."

"I will."

Sander left Mattias to deal with the Ahtissari fallout while he returned to Kalev.

He had a meeting he absolutely did not want to miss.

Chapter Thirteen

"Tell him no, for the third time," a guard snarled into the phone. "Sander is not going to see Paavo."

Chey paused outside the main information room, the center of intelligence gathering and incoming news, when she overheard Sander's name in conjunction with Paavo's. The third brother in the Ahtissari line, the trouble-maker who had nearly killed Sander in a blatant attack years ago and who had wanted to divide Latvala into regions, apparently wanted to see the king. Chey knew that Sander had paid Paavo a visit a year earlier when Paavo began causing problems in jail, and that Paavo had demanded that the king send him to the executioner's chair—or set him free in another country. The latter option hadn't ever been considered, not with Paavo's destructive background, and Sander had denied the execution as well. Chey remembered sitting up with Sander for a week after that conversation, talking through the disturbance it caused in her husband. Having been asked to kill his own sibling, whether Paavo deserved it or not, had hit Sander hard. Chey didn't blame him. It *was* his brother, someone he'd grown up with as a child, and she suspected it was the memory of Paavo in his youth that made the task impossible. Not only that, but Sander, still harboring ill feelings over his attempted murder, refused to give Paavo the easy out. Paavo was paying the price for his actions by being denied that which he most wanted: freedom.

"Excuse me. Is Paavo asking for Sander again?" Chey asked, stepping into the room.

The guard glanced at the door. "He's been demanding to see Sander since this morning. We've informed the guards at the prison it won't happen."

"Did someone inform Paavo that the family seat had been attacked?" Chey knew that word of the attack traveled fast. Perhaps even fast enough to reach inmates in prison.

"Honestly, I don't know. Paavo didn't state a reason, only that he demanded to see Sander immediately." The guard ended the call after a gruff goodbye and hung up the phone.

Chey considered the situation. Paavo might have heard there was an attack but no details. Perhaps he just wanted to rehash his insistence that Sander put him to death or to barter his exile with another country. Either way, Paavo was not a distraction she wanted Sander to have to deal with right now, and it appeared Paavo was going to keep insisting Sander's presence, a thorn in everyone's side. She expected Paavo to pull out all the stops, becoming such a nuisance that Sander would be forced to eventually visit the prison.

After several minutes, she said, "Call them back. Tell him that Sander will see him after all. Then arrange for my transport to the prison." Misinforming Paavo that Sander was coming instead of her would shut him up, at least for the time being.

Every guard in the room stopped what they were doing to snap a look Chey's direction.

"Your Highness--"

"Chey--"

"That's not a good idea--"

Chey interrupted the expected denials.

"Just arrange it. I want to leave as soon as possible." After a moment, she added, "And no, don't call it in first. I'll be there and back before Sander is through with his meeting with Konstantine."

Leaving the guards flustered but moving forward with their new instructions, Chey made her way to the two guards in charge of watching over her children. She didn't mention the mission, only that she was leaving on a brief, important errand and reminded the guards what to do with the kids should anything go wrong at the safe house in her absence. The children were to be put on a plane immediately for Afshar.

Within ten minutes, Chey had a team of three guards ready to escort her through the tunnels. She stepped onto the street at the same place Sander had departed earlier, glancing left and right along the city block before climbing quickly into the waiting Hummer at the curb. All three guards followed her inside.

Minutes later she was on her way to the helipad.

* * *

It was a short trip by air to the prison.

Chey watched the city of Kalev, with its mix of modern buildings and older structures, fade to quaint residential areas and finally, wide open land. The terrain this close to shore was lush as well as rocky, with broad meadows occasionally broken up by large boulders that jutted from the earth like giant teeth. Forests spread out to the north and east, unspoiled by the hand of man.

Miles of beautiful greenbelt passed in a blur, until swaths of open land and meandering rivers took over where the trees left off. It was in one of these exposed areas that the prison housing Paavo stood. The rectangular structure, enclosed in high chain link fencing and rolls of barbed wire, was one of the smaller detention centers of several on Latvala lands. This particular prison had only five hundred cells opposed to thousands at larger facilities. Prisoners of Paavo's status or other high profile inmates were housed here, within easy access of the city but far enough away that should there be a breakout, the guards in one of four towers would see the escapee long before the prisoner could cross the open land to the trees. Any escaped inmate would be forced to hike over rough terrain and miles of exposed land to reach the city.

Once the helicopter landed, two SUVs transported her and the guards to the prison gates, where armed security personnel let them in. The vehicles passed through another gate built into the walls, then stopped in front of an admittance building with wings of the prison jutting off left and right.

Chey disembarked, guards on her heels, and followed an officer through the admittance chamber, through a gated hallway, and into another long hallway to the left. There were no cells here, but rather personnel offices, a medic and other rooms necessary to prison life. The linoleum floors were as polished as a hospital ward, the walls a plain white lacking decoration or architectural nuance. The building was about as utilitarian as any Chey had ever seen. The lighting came from high fixtures locked behind iron grates.

Near the end of the row, at a heavy door with one thick paned window to see in and out, stood no less than four guards. These men wore black and white suits rather than the standard blue and gray uniforms of the other employees.

Arriving, Chey said, "I want to be alone with him."

"Your--"

"Is he secure?"

"Yes."

"Then I'm fine to be alone with you all standing right outside the door." Chey suspected Paavo wouldn't talk anyway with an audience, no matter that any of the guards could look in the window any time.

After a brief discussion between the suits and Chey's own guard, one man opened the door.

Chey drew in a deep breath, girded herself for confrontation, and stepped inside.

It had been multiple years since Chey had laid eyes on Paavo in the flesh, as far back as the birth of her first child. She couldn't have anticipated the changes in Paavo, even if someone had warned her beforehand. Sallow skinned, green eyes brooding in a face gone gaunt, Paavo Ahtissari appeared a beaten man. His short black hair looked as if he had spent considerable time tugging at the strands, making them skew every which way. Although never a big man, standing a couple of inches under six feet, he had lost enough weight to turn his once honed body into a shadow of its former self. The white jumpsuit and slip on shoes did nothing for him, washing out his already compromised complexion. His bony wrists were shackled to a rectangular table designed for the attachment of cuffs, his ankles secured to the legs of a metal chair. When Paavo made eye contact, he scowled.

"Where is my brother? Don't tell me he sent his bitch in his place," Paavo said.

Chey schooled her expression. She approached the table, the only piece of furniture in the room besides Paavo's chair and her own.

"I came of my own accord. Sander is busy." She wanted to see how much Paavo knew about the attack on the family seat, or if he had heard anything at all.

"I *asked* for Sander!" he said, his voice peaking.

"He's busy," she repeated. Chey stood behind the chair for the moment, staring across the table at Paavo. "What is it you want from him now?"

Paavo's jaw clenched and unclenched. He narrowed his eyes. "I demand to see Sander. Now."

"He's not coming."

"Then you've wasted your precious time. I have nothing to say to you when I've made it clear I need to speak to Sander."

"And I'm making it clear that he's not coming. Not today, not tomorrow, not next month or probably next year," Chey retorted in a matter-of-fact tone. "So you talk to me about what you think you need, and I'll either pass it on—or I won't. It just depends how important I think it is."

Fury sparked in Paavo's eyes. He spat curses in his native tongue before switching back to heavily accented English. "I should have slit your throat when I had the chance."

Chey held firm through a shudder that passed down her spine. "Too late. Do you actually have anything serious to say, or should I just leave? I'll make sure to let Sander know he shouldn't bother to stop by in the next five or ten years."

Paavo appeared to weigh his options. His shifty gaze studied Chey's features, as if weighing the measure of her. "I've heard a most unsettling rumor, and I want to know if it's true."

Chey did not step into Paavo's blatant

pause to offer an answer. She wanted him to divulge what he knew—if anything.

He snarled quietly when she didn't offer up details. "Has there, or has there not, been an attack on my home?"

"It's no longer *your* anything, except the place you grew up," Chey reminded him. She didn't delight in pushing his buttons, yet she also didn't hesitate to speak the truth.

"Did it or did it not get attacked!"

"It did."

Paavo waited, sitting forward as if expecting her to go on. When she didn't, he snarled again. "*And?* Do I have to yank the information out of you?"

I'd like to see you try. Chey contained the condescending comment by a spare margin. Instead, she called upon the reserves of calm she had learned during her years as queen. "More than a third of the castle has been damaged."

"Deaths?"

"Many."

"How many?"

"Does the number matter?"

Paavo shouted another curse and banged his cuffed wrists on the table. "You bloody, insipid witch. How many?"

"Eighty-three people."

"Who? Who died?"

"I don't have a list of names."

"My sister? Brothers? Not your kids, or you wouldn't be here. Though you must have been close by, judging from the scrapes and bruises on your face and hands."

Chey couldn't say for sure if that gleam in Paavo's eyes was one of glee at the thought of her being hurt in the attack, or from simply guessing right about the origin of her injuries. Either way, she didn't like it one bit. "Your sister and brothers are all fine. None of them were at the castle when it was attacked."

"But you? You were, were you not?"

Chey did not confirm or deny it. Paavo would probably learn the truth as new details emerged through news outlets and word of mouth.

"What about your children? Where they there as well?" he demanded.

Silence.

"I have a right to know details."

"Is that all you wanted from Sander? You could have asked any of the guards and received the same answer," she said.

"The guards won't tell me much."

"Then how did you hear about the attack?"

"Inmates. I am allowed access to other human beings now and again," he said in a derisive tone.

"Then maybe you can get more details from them, too. But don't keep asking for Sander. He won't be coming. Do I make myself clear? He has no patience for this nonsense, and now that I know you only want to bring him here to put a drain on his time and resources, I'll be sure to tell him not to waste his breath." She turned to the door.

"You didn't fly all the way here just to tell me that. And contrary to your holier-than-thou assertions, I *do* have something else to tell him." He stood from the chair, placed his hands flat on the table, and leaned forward.

Chey paused halfway across the room to look back. She arched a brow, unimpressed with his attempt to loom— or whatever he was doing. It lost effectiveness thanks to his gaunt state.

"I want to offer my help. Who attacked him? I can infiltrate the enemy. Find out their deepest secrets. No one would ever expect to see me, a man sentenced to live out the rest of his days in such luxurious surroundings." He gestured sarcastically to the walls of the prison.

Chey laughed a very quiet laugh. "You can't be serious. Really? That won't happen. Not ever. You've lost touch with whatever snip of reality you had left if you think Sander would trust you again."

"You need to tell him what I said. If the castle has been attacked, and he doesn't know who is responsible, then I can help. I'm a perfect candidate. In times like this, family needs to stick together."

"You're crazy. Get used to these walls, Paavo. You'll die here an old man." Chey, inwardly aghast at the mere thought Paavo expected her to pass on such a ludicrous message, tapped on the door for the guard to let her out.

"It won't stop me from contacting him again. He needs to hear what I have to say, not his ignorant wife who has no right to be queen," Paavo said to her back.

Chey gave the door room to open. She caught a glimpse of a guard on the floor, *her* guard, and a splatter of blood on the far wall. The last thing she saw was the arm of a suited man bringing down the butt of a gun.

Chapter Fourteen

Sander didn't bother to change clothes for his meeting with Konstantine. It didn't matter if he showed up to this private meeting in royal garb or a bath robe. The details would come out the same. He considered all the new information given by Mikel and how he should proceed with Konstantine once they were face to face. It was a delicate balance, treading this line between his responsibility as king and a man bent toward mercenary action when he felt the circumstances warranted it. He wouldn't hesitate to go all out on Konstantine if he had to.

The setting sun hadn't dipped too far into the horizon when Sander stepped out of the limousine and into the hotel's private back entrance. He could have had the helicopter land on the roof of the hotel itself, but that would have drawn the notice of media and citizens on the streets nearby, putting his secretive mission in jeopardy. Three guards flanked his progress, on the lookout for danger.

A long, dim corridor stretched away from the back door, with another, shorter hall branching off to his right. He took the shorter hall to a bank of elevators accessible only by either a key or a passcode that he punched into the keypad. Done in shades of navy blue, silver and gray, the hotel themed itself on the royalty of Latvala, with sweeping architecture reminiscent of the family seat. There were copies of portraits of the Ahtissari lineage in frames in the lobby, as well as photographs of Sander and Chey with the line of princes decorating the walls.

Inside the elevator, half blue and half gray with silver trim, Sander punched the number for the top floor. A floor not just every random citizen could access. He said nothing to his guards on the way up, allowing the men to take the front position in the elevator just in case someone unsavory waited on the other side of the doors when they opened.

The only people in sight when Sander stepped into the foyer were Konstantine's guards. Five of them. They stood on either side of a double set of doors to the suite. More than one man eyed the weaponry Sander wore in the open, on his person, and several started to protest. Sander left the guards to sort out their differences and entered the room. He wasn't about to meet anyone, no matter who, unarmed.

Konstantine paced near a roaring fireplace in a suite built, literally, for a king. A black coat had been tossed over a chair, leaving the king of Imatra in shirtsleeves of white with the tie missing. He had a glass of wine in his hand, a troubled frown on his brow.

Sander closed the door with a thud that snagged Konstantine's attention. The king of Imatra's frown deepened when he saw the weapon belt at Sander's hips.

"Is that really necess--"

"Don't. Just don't," Sander warned Konstantine. "I'm not going anywhere right now without protection. If I wanted you dead—you would be."

Konstantine scowled, then set down his glass. "That's a pretty brazen statement--"

"Let's discuss brazen, shall we?" Sander paced slowly across the room, keeping a glut of gilded furniture between him and Konstantine. There were several other rooms off the main living area, a broad balcony, and a full kitchen that Sander ignored for now. He'd been in this suite before, he knew what it had to offer.

"What we need to discuss, Dare, is how to protect our countries from what is clearly a blatant attack. I *tried* to tell you we shouldn't wait, shouldn't waste time. Now look what's happened." He made an impatient gesture with one hand that apparently indicated all the attacks on their kingdoms.

"I think we should start with the *staged* attacks that *you* arranged near your borders, and how you used corpses to portray your dead soldiers. I'm curious, did you order the bodies blown up, or was that one of your military?" Sander paced, watching Konstantine's expression closely. He was looking for surprise or guilt or some other matching emotion that would give Konstantine away. The flicker of surprise came a moment later, along with a slight widening of Konstantine's eyes. The way the man's posture straightened, as if the king was about to defend himself, told Sander better than words that Mikel hadn't been lying. At least about this. Konstantine tongued his teeth, appearing to consider how to answer.

"Yes, I staged the scene. Yes, I added the Russian flag. I knew I *had* to, because your reputation precedes you, Dare. I knew you wouldn't take the threats against Imatra—against your *own* country—seriously unless you had a lot of provocation. As you can see, we were hit anyway thanks to your lack of support to what should have been *our* cause."

"What you did was show up on my doorstep with false information and make inane demands that no sane king would have agreed upon. It's for this reason that most sovereigns and leaders of nations don't immediately hop to instant decisions, especially when it involves entire countries and the well being of the people. I've learned that *everyone* has an agenda, Konstantine, and it behooves me to take a wait and see attitude. Not only that, but I will not now, nor ever, give up sovereignty of Latvala."

"Instead, you condone our countries being bombed!" Konstantine shouted. "Because that's what you really mean when you sit on your throne of denial and pretend like an attack like this would never happen. You could have prevented this!"

Sander took one threatening step

forward. "You're treading a thin line, Konstantine. Accept the fact that this was out of both of our control. We could have merged all three countries together and it wouldn't have stopped the bombing because you were hell bent on making a statement. You're very lucky I don't haul to to prison right now."

Konstantine's face skewed into a mask of surprise and disbelief. "Wait...what are you suggesting?--"

"I'm suggesting you took your staging one step too far. Arranging a few dead bodies wasn't good enough for you, was it? You needed to bomb Latvala and Somero as extra emphasis to 'help' Thane and I get on board with your idea to take everything over. Although I have to say— bombing your *own* country was really over the top--"

"I did not bomb anyone's country, much less my own! You've lost your mind, Dare."

"I think my mind is intact. You play a good game of cat and mouse, but I don't believe in coincidences where someone happens to attack me so soon after a blatant warning that I would be groveling to their feet if I didn't do as they demanded. You all but admitted you would retaliate, and lo, here we are." Sander spread his hands indicatively, encompassing the bombings as a whole. It was all he could do to remain rational and calm.

Konstantine took a step forward, facing off with Sander. "I'm telling you right now. *I did not bomb anyone.* Not you, not Thane, certainly not myself."

"And I should believe you...why?"

"Because it makes no sense! I had--"

"It makes perfect sense and I just explained why. What I want you to do now, is tell me why I shouldn't haul you to prison and put you on trial for murder?" Sander's patience was beginning to erode despite his best intentions. Flashes of Chey and the children in the devastation of the family seat played behind his eyes, a constant reminder of Konstantine's lies. He didn't have enough proof—yet—to hold Konstantine. Just as he didn't rush to act before, he wouldn't rush to act now. The international complications were great and many regarding the detention of royalty, and he couldn't afford to smear Latavla's name so soon after Paavo turned against his own blood and attempted to overthrow the throne.

Sander had spent years rebuilding the trust of his people. Still. It didn't hurt to let Konstantine know how serious he was about the bombing.

"You wouldn't dare. And it amazes me how you *still* fail to see the consequences of your inaction. We're all going to be taken over, haven't you figured that out? Russia moves against our kingdoms and here you sit, threatening *me*. I would almost say that you *want* to lose Latvala to a greater power."

"Do you have anything at all important to say, Konstantine? I've got other, more important things to do than stand here and listen to you whine. What I do with Latvala is my decision and my decision only. You blaming Russia for the bombings strikes me about as truthful as believing they attacked your border after you staged dead people on the ground. I don't have proof—yet. But I'll find it eventually." Sander forced himself to remain on the other side of the room. He had an irresistible urge to grab Konstantine up by his collar and slam him into the nearest wall.

As if his thoughts alone could manifest into physical action, Konstantine suddenly slumped to the floor. Sander didn't at first understand why the man crumpled in on himself like that. Not until a discrete 'pop' registered a split second after. Diving to the floor, Sander pulled a weapon from the holster to aim at the window, where a neat bullet hole provided proof of what had taken Konstantine down. From his vantage he saw nothing useful; whoever took the shot wasn't inside the suite but across in another building, out of Sander's line of sight. He shouted for the guards, aware in some part of his mind that Konstantine's security might very well take *him* to be the shooter—and shoot in return. He rolled behind a couch out of sight, unwilling to holster his weapon. For all he knew, there were more shooters, or a guard on the shooter's payroll, just waiting to take him out, too.

"Stay down, stay down! Shooter!" Sander called when he heard the door open. "Konstantine's hit!" He wanted to alert his own detail of the threat, make them aware that he hadn't gotten pissed and taken a shot at the king. As well as Konstantine's guard, who probably wouldn't believe him anyway until they saw the hole in the window. Chaos broke out as Sander heard the guards swarm the suite. Men shouted, working through the confusion. His security found him behind the couch before Konstantine's men and Sander urged the guards to stay low.

"Someone call for backup on the street. Cordon off three city blocks and have teams go into the buildings across from the hotel," Sander ordered. One of his men, crouched close by, pulled a cell from his pocket. "Call emergency services, too."

Although from what Sander had glimpsed, no amount of medical aid would save Konstantine. Incredibly, impossibly, an assassination had just occurred on Latvala soil.

* * *

The delicate extraction of Konstantine and Sander did not happen without an increase in tension and a few barbed words thrown back and forth between guards. Sander set the record straight once everyone had made it into the foyer, a better protected area with only one window facing an entirely different angle than from where the shot came. In precise detail, Sander explained what happened. He did not shy away from the terse conversation leading up to the moment when Konstantine had gone down. Medics arrived within minutes, coming in at a crouch, hunkering below the level of the windows—just in case.

Sander refused to leave the building, which was protocol in cases like this, waiting to see if the medics could perhaps work a miracle and save the king. The official time of death rang through the foyer after every attempt to save Konstantine failed.

Departing the hotel under cover of darkness, Sander sank into the back seat of the limousine and pulled out his phone. He muttered vicious curses while he found Chey's number and hit the Call button. There was only so long he could keep a lid on Konstantine's assassination; sooner than later, he knew, word would leak to the media. Already, Konstantine's guards had placed calls to the first in line to the throne of Imatra to inform him that his brother was dead, and he was now king.

The situation couldn't be any worse. Except if the shooter had taken him out, too. Sander thought the only reason he wasn't in a body bag right now was that, upon a brief examination of the window and the room, the guards had discerned that a section of wall had prevented Sander from being shot. He hadn't been standing directly in front of the window at that particular moment.

When Chey's phone went to voicemail, Sander left a message. "Hey, it's me. I wanted to tell you before it hits the news that Konstantine was assassinated while we were having our conversation. I'm all right, I wasn't hit, but he's dead. There isn't any more information to pass along but as soon as I have it, I'll call. Love you."

The next call he made was to Mattias. He explained the entire situation and asked Mattias to pass along the information to Gunnar and Natalia so there wouldn't be any confusion. After, he ordered the driver to take him to a specific address on the outskirts of the city and had another guard call to have someone trustworthy meet them with a change of clothes. Sander couldn't address the media about Konstantine's death armed to the teeth with weapons. Less than twenty minutes later, the limousine pulled up to a house surrounded by wrought iron fencing. After Sander punched in a code on a keypad, the gate rolled back to admit the vehicle. A short driveway led to the front of the imposing Grecian Revival style home, and another drive circled around to the side, delivering the men to an entrance not easily seen from the street. Sander disembarked and, with his guards surrounding on every side, made the brief journey to a door he opened by entering more numbers into a second keypad. Three guards went in first to secure the elegantly furnished home. Sander had purchased it, along with several others, after the last situation with Paavo. He'd needed secure places to go on a moment's notice other than destinations like the bunker, which was about as safe as safe could get—unless someone on the inside sold Sander out. So he'd invested in myriad residences only he knew about, places he would use once or twice before selling to buy something else.

The extra caution had paid off.

Dressed in white marble with baby blue and beige accents, the interior of the home sprawled three floors. Tall columns dotted the lower level and cathedral windows allowed maximum sun glow during daylight hours. At night, like now, the windows were shuttered against the blackness where anyone might hide and take shots from the yard.

While his guards secured the house and took up defensive positions, Sander went into a downstairs office and nudged the door halfway closed with his foot. Snapping on a light, he scrubbed his hands over his face and exhaled a long breath.

Everything he thought he knew about Konstantine and Imatra had just been dealt a lethal blow. Positive that Konstantine had ordered the bombings, Sander couldn't figure out why Konstantine himself had been assassinated. If he'd orchestrated the attacks and the explosions, why was Konstantine a target? Second guessing every thought he'd had since day one, Sander sank into a leather chair behind a somewhat plain but sturdy desk. Sparsely filled bookcases lined the walls, flanking a cold fireplace with a mirror above the mantel.

Forced to rethink the Russian angle, Sander considered all his options. Perhaps there *was* a contingent who had been threatening Konstantine from the beginning. Konstantine might have had poor judgement when he staged the attacks, but maybe, just maybe, his paranoia had gotten the better of him and in his mind, there was no other way than to up-play the danger to himself and his country. Just because he wouldn't have done it that way, and didn't agree with Konstantine's tactics, didn't mean the threat itself from Russia wasn't real.

Cursing under his breath, he stared at a far wall, going over all the events leading to this moment in time. He needed to be preparing a statement to the media but he couldn't stop the influx of conflicting ideas once they'd started.

One thing he *did* know, was that attacks were happening in tandem, methodically, with pre-thought out precision. Someone had taken the time to do this in a certain order, though what the end game was, Sander didn't know. Perhaps the Russians wanted all three countries, as Konstantine had thought, and were making a collective move for a take-over.

That meant the entire country of Latvala needed to prepare for war. He loathed the thought of making the announcement to the people on the heels of discussing Konstantine's assassination. It was the responsible thing to do, however, in light of the recent developments.

His problem was that he still had no *solid* proof that the Russian's had even crossed the border. There were attacks—staged initially by Konstantine—and bombings in three different countries, along with Konstantine's death. Yet, thus far, there had been no word from the Russians. No new demands, no news to his kingdom or Thane's. Sander imagined the Russians would be doing more now than sending letters in the wake of such blatant attacks.

That was the one thing that stayed Sander's hand. As he had told Konstantine, hadn't acted earlier for the same reason—a lack of hard proof. Sander had learned bitter lessons in his life about reacting to things that *seemed* to be, rather than what *was.* If he came out on live television and blamed the Russians, he might be precipitating a confrontation he wouldn't win.

While he waited for the new guards to arrive, Sander picked up the phone on the desk. He needed second, third and fourth opinions about how to proceed before making any kind of public statement.

The last thing he needed was an all out panic.

Chapter Fifteen

An ache in her neck brought Chey up from the dregs of sleep. She lifted her head, groaning when another, sharper stab of pain lanced through her skull. Disoriented, she pried her lashes open to see a room bare of furniture except a desk she sat in front of and an empty chair across from her own. A smear of blood on the chair discolored the silver metal. Chey wondered whose it was.

She recalled then that she had been on the way out of the room—she was at the prison—when someone hit her over the head. Blinking several times to help clear her vision, she looked side to side, half expecting to see Paavo dead on the floor. A bright streak of blood, as if a body had been dragged toward the hallway, marred the pristine linoleum.

No body. At least not in this room.

She recalled downed guards in the hall, with blood spattered on the wall, just before she'd blacked out. Tugging on the rope that bound her wrists, chafing her skin in the process, she struggled to get free.

What the hell was going on? Someone had attacked the prison and kept her alive for reasons she didn't immediately understand. Unless it was Konstantine's doing. Maybe he'd had her followed. Why kill Paavo, then, and not her? Did Konstantine consider Paavo to be useless since the prince held no emotional weight with Sander any longer? Chey knew she was a better bargaining chip with Sander simply because she was his wife.

The lack of voices in the hallway was an ominous portent. Her guards were dead, they had to be, or she would have already been released.

Staring at the streak of blood on the ground, she twisted her hands, pulling upward and outward, biting back noises of pain. Her vision swam with the effort, no doubt exacerbated by the blow to her head.

She had to get free and find a phone.

* * *

"What?" Sander answered his cell phone with more abruptness than he

215

meant to. It had been a long hour of conversations with advisors and his brothers and he wanted to take another call like he wanted another hole in his head.

"Your Majesty, the media is growing restless--"

Sander cut Urmas off. "Yes, I know. They're already here. My men have them set up in a meeting room down the hall. I'll get to the announcement when I'm good and ready."

Undaunted by Sander's terse replies, Urmas said, "Leaders from other countries are calling by the dozen. What should I tell them?"

"It'll have to wait. Tell them I'm in meetings and I'll get back to them when I can." Sander needed pain medication for the enormous headache blooming behind his eyes. There was one more call he needed to make, however, before he did anything else. He dialed Ahsan from his cell phone rather than the landline.

"I don't like what I'm hearing coming out of Latvala right now," Ahsan said by way of hello. The lilt of his mid-eastern accent was mild and easy to understand.

"Yes, it's been a night over here. To make matters worse, I have serious doubts about the Russian angle, yet after Konstantine's death, they're the most likely suspect." Sander could tell Ahsan his suspicions without fear of the man saying anything to the media.

"My offer still stands. If you need anything, you have only to ask."

"Actually, that's one reason I'm calling. I think I'm going to send Chey and the kids to Afshar. Just to be on the safe side. There is too much about all this I don't understand."

"Do you want me to send my jet, so you can have yours at your disposal? You may need to depart the country in a hurry."

"Thanks, yes. Let me set it up with Chey and the guards and I'll text you when it's good to send the plane over." Sander hated separating from his family at at time like this, but he was still smarting from the attack at Ahtissari castle and wouldn't risk their safety again. Not with bombers and shooters on the loose.

"Just let me know. Are you sure you don't want me to come over? Chey and the kids will be safe here at my home without my presence."

Sander seriously considered the offer.

Ahsan, in position of absolute power in his country, was one of the best people to ask for advice. He understood what was at stake regarding country and sovereignty—and consequence.

"I'll tell you what. Give me tonight to see if I can come up with some answers. If there are more attacks or I receive a formal letter of responsibility, I'll call you right away."

"Excellent. Hey—watch your back, brother."

Sander smiled a grim smile. "Thanks. Talk to you soon."

Pocketing the cell phone, Sander stood from the chair and plucked his suit coat off a peg. He'd changed from war gear to formal attire for the announcement he needed to make. Striding into the hall, Sander passed several members of security on his way to the small media room. He hadn't ever intended it to be used for this purpose, but the spare furniture arrangement left room for the three reporters and their three cameramen. Cream colored walls made a decent backdrop.

"Your Majesty! Can you tell us--"

Sander held up a hand to stop the deluge before it began. He'd invited only three of the most prominent stations to this destination, not because he wanted to dodge questions from a larger group, but because the more people who knew about this once secret residence, the greater the chance of a strike against him.

"I'm going to make a statement only. The reason is that I don't have all the answers yet," he explained, to make it clear to the reporters that they were there to deliver his message and that was it. Tugging the edges of his coat into neater lines, he did up two buttons and took his place in front of the cameras. He was as ready as he would ever be. "Let's get started."

Chapter Sixteen

Chey winced as the ropes tore at her sensitive skin. Her effort paid off; the bindings fell away from her hands. Surging to her feet, she rubbed feeling back into her forearms and fingers and sought something, anything, to use as a weapon. The chairs were too heavy and bulky, the table too unwieldy. Made of metal, she couldn't even break off a leg to use like a baton. That left the rope.

Something, she told herself, was better than nothing.

Grasping the whip-thin binding, she clutched it in her hand with a loop extending from the fist of her fingers. If all else failed, she would use it like a crop to beat against an attacker's face. She spent a moment patting her pockets for her phone, which she did not find. Someone had remembered to strip it from her before leaving her tied to the chair.

Opening the door, surprised to find the attackers hadn't barricaded her in, she stepped cautiously into the hall. Just as she remembered from her glimpse, there were downed guards scattered on the floor. All four of her own, blood leaking from beneath their bodies, as well as one of the suited guards that had been standing outside when she'd arrived. Chey didn't see the other three and guessed they were dead in another hallway. Making her way around a puddle of blood, hurting inside at the needless death that choked the corridor, she bent near the first body and sought a weapon. She needed a gun. Or a phone. After a brief search, finding nothing, she moved on to the second guard. And the third. Each man had been stripped of all personal belongings. Moving further along the hall, she crouched next to the suited man, listening for sounds of movement in all directions. The only thing she heard besides her own labored breathing was a faint hum that might have been air pushing through the ducts.

The last guard had no weapons, no identification, no phone.

"Dammit," Chey whispered. Whoever had attacked the prison made sure to leave nothing of use behind. Not even keys, which she needed to get past the gate at the end. Chey tested the bars on the iron door, cringing inwardly when the gate clacked against itself, sending a sharp echo through the next corridor.

Backtracking, she went to the other end where another door blocked her escape. This door was a regular door, with a knob and a lock. A door that didn't budge when she banged against it with her shoulder. Of course. The doors in the prison were no doubt extra fortified in case of an inmate break-out. One by one, she entered each room along the hall—those that were open, with doors unlocked—and searched for a phone. The lack of anything except plain desks and chairs suggested these were meeting and conference rooms used for other inmate visitations.

In the fourth room, Chey found several tables, vending machines, a small counter top with a coffee maker and a microwave. No landlines, not even a small refrigerator where she might find water. She needed a drink to wet her dry throat.

"You were always good at getting away," Paavo said from the doorway.

Startled, Chey flipped around, one hand over her heart, the other gripping the rope. Paavo, whom she thought to be dead, was very much alive. And, she noted with shock, looked nothing like he had when she'd seen him last. His skin was still on the pale side but not sallow, his hair styled neatly away from his face. A fine suit of navy pinstripes replaced the utilitarian white jump suit, though his body was as gaunt as it had been earlier. That part was not an illusion. He almost resembled the prince she remembered meeting all those years ago on her initial visit to Latvala. This Paavo was not as vibrant, as if prison life had sucked out his charisma, his soul. Those were dead eyes staring back at her.

"Nothing to say?" he said with an arched brow. "That will change soon enough. Why don't you have a seat?"

Chey tried to make the right connections. Paavo had somehow organized this. He was responsible for the dead guards, both her own and one guarding his door. The hows and whys escaped her.

"Or you can stand. You'll answer my questions either way." Paavo casually leaned a shoulder into the doorframe and pocketed his hands, as if he had nothing better to do, or nowhere to go.

"What questions are those?" she asked,

keeping a small table and one chair between her and the prince.

Paavo's lips quirked. "I want to know where Sander is."

Chey's cheek twitched. "I don't know."

"I think you do."

"I don't know where he is, Paavo. I left to come here and he went somewhere else. You know how this game is played. Sander doesn't tell me sensitive information—especially when there has been a bombing—so that I *can't* tell should someone take me captive." That wasn't always true, and certainly not true today, but her internal warning system demanded she not to give Paavo any more information than she had to.

"But you were somewhere with him before you left to come here," he pointed out. Then, he added, "You can make this easy or hard, Chey. I don't recommend the hard way, myself."

Chey knew he was trying to scare her into confession. And he might not be bluffing, she reminded herself. Paavo might very well torture her to get the information he wanted. Rather than give him an answer, she asked, "You're responsible for the bombings, aren't you?"

"Where is he? His holding away from the city? The little cabin in the woods that used to belong to father? The safe house in Kalev, with the bunkers he always thinks will save him?"

It took all Chey's control not to twitch or flinch when Paavo mentioned the bunkers. Of course he would know they existed. He knew the more intimate hiding places for royalty, considering he was one of them. "How did you do it? You've been in a special cell here, I know, with limited interaction. How did you plan an attack from inside prison?"

He wanted information from her, and Chey wanted information in return. She overcame the shock that wanted to linger at Paavo's deception, forcing herself to think about possible ways to escape. As he'd said—she had a knack for getting out of tight situations. Sometimes on her own, other times with a little help.

Paavo straightened and stepped back into the corridor. He murmured to someone Chey couldn't see. Sweat popped out on her forehead from a sudden surge of fear. He wouldn't be so easily drawn into answering her questions and, she discovered, was quite serious about her answering his own. Three men rounded into the room, attired in uniforms that Chey knew were not of the Latvala military. Navy jackets with red swatches on the front, matching pants and white gloves were a stark change from Latvala's color schemes of navy, silver, dove gray and white.

Russians. These men were Russian. Yet it was a Latvala accent that fell from one man's tongue when he said, "It's better if you don't fight."

Russia wasn't invading Latvala at all. Nor Imatra. Paavo was using his own men, dressed as someone else, to throw the scent off his trail. To point blame at another, probably innocent country. As far as she could tell, his plan was working to perfection. Sander had his doubts about the Russians, however, and she found herself endlessly glad that her husband was so cautious. He might have started a war that ended with half of Latvala blown off the map.

Maybe that was Paavo's plan all along. Use someone else's military by proxy to do most of his dirty work. Maybe, too, he'd sold himself out to the Russians. She couldn't be sure.

The rope in her fingers slithered to the floor.

Grasping the back of the nearest chair, she picked it up and launched it at the closest guard. The chair bounced to the floor after the man blocked it with a hand. Chey upturned the table, next, scrambling away from the three uniformed guards as they darted forward, coming from all sides. Reaching down, she snatched up the rope again and wielded it like a whip, lashing out at the men's faces. Landing a few shots, which drew snarls and growls from the guards, she stumbled forward when one caught the loop and pulled her off balance.

"No, no!" She fought against their trapping hands, using a foot to kick at one man's shin. Arms wrenched behind her back, two guards pushed her toward the door, toward Paavo who watched impassively from the hall.

Scowling, Chey said, "You won't get away with it. Just like the last time. Sander will figure it out."

Paavo looked unintimidated."Probably. But not in time to stop me—or to save you."

* * *

Sander exited the conference room

after delivering his speech, ignoring the incessant questions the reporters asked even though he'd already told them he would be making a statement only. Leaving the reporters behind, he stalked through the foyer, pausing once to ask one of his guards to escort the reporters from the property.

This particular safe house wasn't safe any longer. Or wouldn't be, once the reporters hit the streets. It hadn't mattered that he'd specifically requested the media say nothing to anyone—he knew he couldn't trust their word or trust, too, that the enemy wouldn't find the reporters and extract the information in unpleasant ways.

As he loosened his tie, he withdrew his phone and tried Chey's cell again. When he remembered that she probably wasn't getting service underground, he called the landline at the bunker instead.

"Yes?" someone answered on the other end.

"Find Chey and put her on the phone, please." He hadn't had contact with her for hours and he needed to update her about the trip to Afshar. The sooner he got his family to Ahsan's stronghold, the better.

"She's not here, your Majesty."

Sander frowned. "What do you mean she's not there?"

"She left earlier today."

"*What?*" Sander came to a stop in the foyer. Mattias and Leander, standing with a group of guards near the door, glanced his way.

"She left earlier, your Majesty. Paavo had been leaving messages for you and she ordered the helicopter to take her to the prison. She's not back yet."

"How long has she been gone?" he bellowed. He met Mattias's eyes, then Leander's, and stalked out of the foyer. Mattias and Leander fell into step at his side.

"Four hours or so. Maybe a little longer."

Seething, Sander ripped off the tie and tossed it aside. He gestured to the side door, indicating he wanted Mattias to have someone get a car ready. To Leander, he said, "Find the five best fighters and bring them with us."

"You got it." Leander pivoted back toward the foyer. Mattias parted off to instruct the guards they would be leaving shortly.

While Sander began coming out of his

suit, he said, "Didn't anyone think to call me before now? Why was she allowed to go to the prison in the first place?"

"Sorry, your Majesty. She decided at the last second, and we thought she'd be back long before now."

"Yes, *why* isn't she back? I want you to leave me on the line and have someone else call the prison." In his borrowed room, Sander shucked his formal clothing for the preferred gear of black. Pants, shirt, vest, weapon belt and shoulder holster.

"We don't know why she's not back. Someone's on the line to the prison. No answer so far."

Of course not, Sander fumed to himself. Tucking the phone against his ear and shoulder, he sat on the end of the bed to pull his combat boots on and yank the laces tight. "Keep trying. Someone has to answer."

The news that no one was answering the main line at the prison worried him. Someone should be manning the desk at all times. Checking his weapons and stash of ammunition, Sander exited the room.

"Still no answer, your Majesty."

Sander didn't bother with goodbyes. He

ended the call and marched toward the side exit just as Leander approached with five guards following in his wake.

"Check your weapons, make sure you have extra back up," Sander said. "We're going to the prison and I don't know what to expect when we get there."

"The prison?" Mattias said, leading the procession out to a pair of Hummers. "Why the prison?"

"Chey's there," he said, splitting off to the lead Hummer. Mattias and Leander followed him, along with one guard. The other four diverted to the secondary vehicle.

"Why is she at the prison?" Mattias asked as he settled into the back seat.

"Apparently Paavo's been asking for me again. You know how he does. He demands my presence, I ignore him. I couldn't tell you why she went, but no one is answering at the front desk. Which just makes no sense." Sander stared out at the darkness beyond the windows. The temperature was dropping again, forcing citizens on the street to bundle up. Large manor houses sat behind wrought iron fencing, some of the structures resembling sentinels with their windows lit from within.

"I agree. I don't understand why she went," Mattias said.

Sander called Gunnar next. His brother answered on the second ring.

"What's going on, Sander?" Gunnar said, foregoing hello.

"I need you to go to the bunker in Kalev. Get there as fast as you can. Take my kids and the three guards you trust the most and get them out of there."

"Why, what happened?"

"Just do it, Gunnar. Take an SUV and drive around the back roads close to the airport in Kalev, but don't go there until someone texts you that the plane is ready and waiting. Stay on the move, and try not to scare the crap out of my kids. They've been through a lot."

"All right. I'm on my way."

"If Chey calls you or Krislin for any reason, please tell her to call me or one of you call me, okay?" Krislin, Gunnar's wife, was a good friend of Chey's. Sander wanted to cover all his bases in case Chey got word out to someone other than himself.

"I'll tell her. Don't worry about the kids. I'll make sure they're safe."

"Thanks. I'll update you soon." Sander ended that call and made another to get the private jet fueled and a flight plan in place. He didn't have time to wait for Ahsan to send a plane all the way from Afshar.

"There's a delay with the helicopter," the driver said. He'd been on his own phone, making arrangements.

"What delay?"

"The one that went to the prison is still there, but the pilot isn't responding. And the other chopper is all the way in Vogeva. I ordered it back here as soon as possible."

Sander clenched his teeth. There were few reasons the pilot wouldn't respond to a direct call. Crashing the chopper was one of them. He couldn't contemplate the implications of someone shooting the craft down. *Wouldn't.* There was something else going on, a miscommunication or misunderstanding. He cursed under his breath.

The last thing he needed was a delay in his own flight. Driving would take too long. He said, "Get one here, I don't care if we have to commandeer a media helicopter to do it."

"Yes, your Majesty."

Sander dialed Chey's phone. No answer.

Chapter Seventeen

In the same chair she'd been tied to before, Chey stared across the room at Paavo, ignoring the burn on her wrists from a fresh length of rope binding her hands tight. The prince paced near the wall, posture lax, hands still in his pockets. As if he didn't have a care in the world.

"I did say that you shouldn't take the hard road, Chey," Paavo finally said.

"Just get your torture over with already. I'm not going to tell you where he is because *I don't know.*"

"See, rushing takes the fun—and anticipation—out of things. You forget that I remember how tough you can be sometimes, and that torturing you would likely take a long time thanks to your stubborn streak and penchant for holding off pain. Torturing *you* would be a waste."

Chey stiffened in her seat. She hadn't missed his emphasis on her. Suddenly she fretted that Paavo had someone she cared for in custody: a best friend, an in-law, one of her staff. Knowing that her refusal to cooperate would result in someone else's harm made her stomach churn.

"Your mind is hard at work now, isn't it?" Paavo asked. "You're wondering who, if not you, I would consider hurting."

Chey said nothing.

"No questions? No guesses?"

She remained silent. Her insides twisted with fear and anxiety. She didn't want to be responsible for someone else's pain.

"Not even one?"

Chey fought off the urge to rant at Paavo. He was doing this on purpose, trying to get under her skin. And it was working.

"How about this. How about—you tell me where Sander *was,* if not where he is, and I'll reconsider sparing Elias's life."

Her children's names were the very last she expected to hear come out of Paavo's mouth. Rage replaced fear, forcing her to sit forward in the chair. "Don't you dare touch my son!"

The corner of Paavo's mouth twitched upward. "I've got your attention now, haven't I? Tell me where Sander was when you saw him last." Coins and keys jangled in Paavo's pockets when his fingers brushed against them.

"How can you even think of hurting a child? He's innocent, a baby. You wouldn't stoop so low, not even you, Paavo, to torture your own nephew." Chey's voice shook, as did her hands.

"And yet, you still haven't answered the question." Paavo clicked his tongue, as if chiding her. Warning her.

Chey considered her options. She could tell Paavo where she'd seen Sander last, putting not just her husband in jeopardy, but also her kids, who were being held in the same place. Or she could lie, putting everyone in jeopardy when Paavo sent someone to check a fake, distant locale only to discover Sander and the kids weren't there. The latter option might buy her more time, however. Might buy Sander and her kids more time. She wasn't positive Paavo didn't already have her kids in his custody, though, even if she didn't see how it was possible. Clearly, he had been plotting and planning for a very long time, and had inside help to accomplish all that he had accomplished. He might have attacked the bunker, taken her kids, but found Sander missing.

He met her eyes across the room, a knowing look in his own. "Thinking over which option is best, hm? You apparently don't take the threat seriously enough."

"No, that's not it. I'm just...shocked. I can't believe you've somehow managed all this from prison." Chey realized she shouldn't be as surprised as she was. Paavo had tried to end Sander once—and had nearly succeeded. Was it so far of a stretch to know he'd either joined with other forces or used a fake foe to try and gain his freedom? For the last three years, Paavo had done everything in his power to get Sander to execute him or exile him to another country. Being behind bars was a special kind of torture that Paavo didn't want to endure. He would have rather been dead—according to him. The whole time he'd had an alternate course of action. Sander had spent endless hours attempting to heal the people of Latvala, but there *were* contingents that still believed in the ideals Paavo had presented during his coup. People who supported him despite the fact that Paavo would have turned on them once he'd taken the throne.

"It wasn't as difficult as you might

imagine."

"But...how did you get contact with the Russians? Or is that all a ruse? Did you use their uniforms to throw people off, to cast suspicion somewhere else and create havoc while your people planted bombs?" Chey couldn't stop the questions once they started. She had a desperate need to know how Paavo had done it.

"The Russians had nothing to do with any of this. I long to know if Sander considered attacking the country." He paused to arch a questioning brow.

"You know how Sander is. He's over the top cautious." Desperate to distract Paavo and keep his mind off hurting her children, Chey strove hard to engage Paavo about the semantics of his plan.

"Indeed. It's very possible he'll follow through now that Konstantine is dead, however. Who is left to blame other than the Russians?"

Chey drew in a breath. Konstantine was dead?

"Oh, caught you by surprise, yes? Then again, you *have* been a little busy the last few hours, unable to get updates about the escalation."

"Konstantine is dead? Why? I don't--"

"I see no harm in telling you. You won't

be able to pass any of this on, anyway." Paavo paused, then said, "By the way. Every minute you make me wait for an answer is a strike against you—and against your family. Just because I'm chatting you up doesn't mean I've forgotten my threat. We're through Elias and into Emily--"

"The last time I saw Sander he was in the hinterlands, searching for Russian contingents along the border. All I know is that he had a small team and intended to do spot checks, looking for incursions." Chey forgot the details of Paavo's ultimate plan in favor of trying to save her children. She lied through her teeth, hoping, praying, that Sander had noticed her missing by now and would take immediate action. She knew Sander *had* been at the border, doing exactly as she'd said he'd been doing, except the timeline was off. She didn't stray from Paavo's eye contact, attempting to sell him on the 'truth' by not backing down.

"Isn't that convenient. He's somewhere I can't locate him, even though I know where he is. I wonder, Chey, if you're really telling me the truth. It will take considerable time to do a thorough search. Almost, but not quite, like looking for a needle in a haystack."

"You wanted to know where he was—that's where. He won't attack Russia until he's exhausted all other possibilities, and manually checking the border was high priority." Oh God, Chey thought, let him believe me.

"What you don't apparently know is that Sander was with Konstantine when he was assassinated, which places Sander in the city a handful of hours ago. So either you're lying, or Sander was recalled to Kalev to meet with Konstantine after you left to come here." Paavo paced the room, a slow meander, staring at the floor in consideration.

Chey's stomach flipped over. Paavo knew more than he was telling, had from the beginning, and he'd baited her to see if she would tell the truth, or lie. What were her options? To out her husband's whereabouts, and thus her kids, was tantamount in her eyes to signing their death certificate. Lying had been her only recourse.

"Nothing to say?" Paavo slanted her a sly look.

"I'm wondering why you didn't get Sander, too, if he's your ultimate target. If he was with Konstantine, then why aren't you gloating about Sander's death as well?"

"Unfortunately, he was out of the sniper's line of sight. What a stroke of luck for Sander, or he *would* be dead right now." Paavo glanced at the door when a guard knocked, then let himself in. He held up Chey's ringing phone, as if indicating Paavo would be interested in the caller.

Chey breathed through her panic. She watched Paavo cross the room, take the phone, and smile when he glanced at the screen. He pivoted and advanced on her, extending the phone.

"You're going to find out where Sander is right now. Don't get cute, Chey, you're already down two kids. It won't take much to add Erick to the list." He pressed a button and held the phone to her ear.

Steeling her resolve, trying to collect her thoughts, Chey said, "Sander, I swear to God, you better have a damn good reason why you haven't called before now."

* * *

Alarm bells went off in Sander's head when he heard the vehemence in Chey's voice. He gestured to the driver to pull over to the side of the road, lessening the background noise. He tilted the phone so Mattias and Leander, who had suddenly leaned forward in their seats, could hear the conversation. Sander knew right away that Chey was in trouble. He had to think quick. Her immediate accusation was a 'sign', a code they'd worked on together after the last fiasco with his brother. A way to communicate with each other, to warn each other, without tipping off people nearby.

"You should check your messages more often. I left several. Where are you and why aren't you with the kids?" Sander listened for any telltale sounds that would help him place Chey's whereabouts. She had been at the prison, but that didn't mean she was still there.

"Don't worry about where *I* am. Where are *you?*"

Mattias leaned into Sander's line of sight, shaking his head *no.*

"We had to move the command center. Konstantine's dead, so I didn't feel safe at the bunker any longer. Where are you? We need that helicopter, Chey." Sander waited to see if Chey would persist in asking him where the command center had moved to. Under normal circumstances, in a case like this, she wouldn't ask him specifics over an open line. Not when the family seat had been bombed and people were being murdered. If she did, then he knew her safety had been compromised. Someone had her under their control.

"I'm about to head back from Pallan island. I needed a few things from Kallaster. Where should I tell the pilot to go?"

Leander and Mattias started making rapid hand gestures from the back seat. Sander couldn't decipher anything at first, then understood the mouthed word *ruins.* There were quite a few sets of ruins in Latvala, old castles from his forebears that had become mostly unlivable. He needed to draw off whoever was with Chey, lead them deep into the out-country, away from the city and the citizens.

"Remember the Ruins of Amsler? We're using that as our headquarters now. It's in decent enough shape but way off the grid, somewhere no one will think to look. The pilot will know where to go." Sander picked a ruin that afforded him and his men a place to hide outside the castle itself. There were outbuildings and forest to take cover in. He listened as black static hissed down the line when Chey momentarily went quiet.

"I think I remember. That one castle I really liked, the one with the crumbling turret?"

"That one." He paused, then asked, "You okay, Chey?"

Another, smaller hesitation. "Yes. I have...I have some bad news though. Urmas didn't want me to tell you until I saw you, but I think you should know now."

Sander frowned. He knew Urmas hadn't been in touch with Chey. Not for hours. "What?"

"Paavo. He's...dead."

Chapter Eighteen

Chey studied Paavo's face as he mouthed the words again. *Tell him I'm dead.* She licked her lips, and repeated herself. "Paavo's gone, Sander."

"What? Wait...how the hell did that happen?"

"We just got the news. Urmas said there's been an attack at the prison. A lot of inmates were involved." Chey made the story up as she went, taking smaller cues from Paavo. She knew Sander understood her warning, knew that he'd come up with the ruins as a place to draw her—and whoever was with her—out. She wasn't sure Sander knew it was Paavo, especially not after Paavo made her lie. There was no help for it. Sander cursed over the line.

"Are you sure, Chey?" he finally said.

"Yes. Urmas had no doubt. I'm not sure what kind of attack, whether it was an invasive force or a mutiny, but he's gone."

"All right. I'll meet you at the ruins. And Chey—I love you."

"I love you, too." Chey winced when Paavo snatched the phone from her ear. Tracking Paavo's progress across the room, she watched him pass on a quiet message to his men. No matter what else happened now, Sander at least knew there was a problem and would act accordingly. While Paavo no doubt plotted Sander's demise, Chey plotted *his*. She considered all the actions between the prison and the ruins that Paavo would have to take—the drive to the helicopter, the flight, the approach to the ruins—and where she might trip him up. She was far from helpless, here.

Paavo turned back, sliding the phone into his pocket. He brought up a gun. Aimed it her way. "You have been very useful. Thank you."

Chey's eyes widened. Shock stunned her mind. She never heard the bullet that hit her high in the chest, sending a bloom of pain spiraling out from the impact.

* * *

"What do we know?" Leander said the moment Sander ended the call. He ticked items off on his fingers. "We know Konstantine received a letter from a Russian commander about consequences if he didn't allow Imatra to be absorbed by Russia. All three of our countries were subsequently bombed, and Konstantine was executed. Konstantine might have staged some of the smaller skirmishes, and *maybe* he arranged for bombs, but he sure as hell didn't put a hit out on himself. We haven't heard a thing from the Russians ourselves, and now someone—who wants to get their hands on you next—has Chey. The prison never sent out any distress signals, so someone has taken control from the officers there. Paavo is apparently dead, maybe done the same way as Konstantine, yet we've received no correspondence demanding that you allow Latvala to be absorbed into the Russian fold, no one accepting responsibility for their actions. Only suspicious letters and rumors. What ifs. Nothing about this adds up. We would have known if Russian troops penetrated as far as the prison and we haven't heard anything from our military about any incursions. Who the hell had the plan and the power to wrest control from that many armed guards?"

Sander listened as Leander spelled out the situation in black and white. He gestured for the driver to get back on the road. He forced down an urgent sense of foreboding to concentrate on the problem. The news that Paavo was dead somehow didn't seem real. "I don't know. Maybe a smaller group—but that's a pretty heavily armed building. You'd think we would have heard *something* from someone before they went down."

"Exactly," Mattias said. He set a hand on Sander's shoulder, a silent show of support and understanding. "I don't think we're dealing with Russians. I don't think they're about to invade three countries for a take over."

"I agree. It's something else. A more personal strike, and I'm not entirely sure Konstantine was ultimately the prime target," Leander added. "So then we have to go over who your most volatile enemies are, Sander, and figure out who had the motivation to take it this far."

"We've made great strides toward peace with pretty much everyone. Yeah, I've got enemies in the elite ranks of the world, but why begin with Imatra? Why draw anyone else into it at all if it was me they wanted all along? Thane took a hit, too.

His involvement and Konstantine's death don't make sense. It has to be related somehow." Sander paused to make several more calls. He ordered the closest military members to the Ruins of Amsler, instructed no less than ten snipers to get up in the trees around the castle and into the castle itself. His brief conversation with Urmas confirmed his worst fears: Urmas hadn't had any contact at all with Chey in the last six or seven hours. The liaison was shocked to hear Paavo was dead, hadn't heard a breath of the rumor from anyone at the castle. Which meant Chey had made the lie up on the fly, for reasons Sander couldn't guess. After he ended the call, he said, "Urmas didn't know anything about Paavo."

"Think Chey's trying to send us a message there?" Leander asked.

"Maybe. She had to know that she didn't talk to Urmas, and that I would call him to confirm or deny. So she lied about who told her of Paavo's death--" Sander stalled. He felt as if the answer was close at hand, as if his mind wanted to make the final connections yet the truth remained elusive.

"What is it, Dare?" Mattias asked, harking back to the childhood nickname

Sander's siblings sometimes used.

"I don't know. I feel like the answer is right here, that we're overlooking something obvious. Or that we should know how to figure it out. Someone had to have infiltrated the ranks of the officers at the prison--" Sander paused again. The dark landscape drew his gaze. He could see the outline of his grim refection in the window, the stern set of his mouth and the twitch of a muscle in his jaw.

"What are you thinking?" Mattias asked.

"Infiltration," Sander said.

"And?"

"Who has everything to hold against me, who's already on the inside? Who could have attacked from *within* the prison, rather than without?" Dread settled heavy in Sander's chest.

"Paavo," Leander and Mattias said at the same time.

Sander said nothing for a full minute. "I don't pretend to understand what the hell Konstantine and Imatra have to do with anything, but as far as the prison goes, Paavo makes sense to me."

"Maybe he tried to make a deal with Konstantine, then had him assassinated when he thought the king was no longer valuable," Leander said.

"Or just in the way," Mattias added, sounding as grim as Sander looked.

"I could be way off base," Sander said. "I guess we'll find out when we reach the ruins." He started checking all his weaponry, even though he'd done it before he left the bunker. It kept his hands busy while his mind churned through possibilities. They might be set upon by Russian troops for all Sander knew—or he could be right, and Paavo would show with whatever force he'd developed while in prison. He remembered the meetings when Paavo had begged him for an execution date and, barring that, demanded that he send him overseas somewhere to start a new life. A prison cell was wasting away Paavo's soul, according to his brother. Sander had refused, of course, because Paavo deserved the punishment after all the lives he'd taken. He wouldn't give Paavo the easy way out, much to Paavo's discontent and fury.

Now, Paavo might be seeking revenge, or he could have finally gotten the release he craved.

Sander only hoped his brother didn't take Chey down with him.

Chapter Nineteen

The Ruins of Amsler towered above the rocky landscape, flanked by trees on three sides. One of the four turrets had begun to collapse, with a growing pile of old stones building at the base. The castle lacked a surround, though its walls were tall and an enormous wooden door made penetration of the interior difficult. High windows provided a sweeping view of the landscape in all directions, the depressions resembling rectangular black holes in the darkness.

Sander ordered the driver to take a back road in, one not well traveled or known by most, and left the SUV in a small clearing toward the back of the property. There were no other residences within a three mile radius, only a handful of outbuildings that were in far worse shape than the castle itself. An outdoor kitchen, stables, brewery and bake house were barely recognizable for their former intended purpose. Sander had considered renovating or fortifying the ruins that dotted Latvala, a move purely driven by the desire to preserve the history. Thus far, he'd not started any of those projects. Therefore, Amsler remained cold and stark, a monolith slowly wilting to the decay of time. Once upon an age, his ancestors had thrived here. Kings had conducted the rise of Latvala, battling back enemies while their wives gave birth to future generations.

The current king skulked through the forest with his men spread out around him, weapons drawn. Although Sander had his suspicions about the culprit of the attacks, he progressed through the trees, on alert for anything. For Russians, foreign assailants, and his own brother. Mattias, Leander and the driver circled the perimeter, clearing the immediate grounds of intruders. Leander stole through a back entrance into the castle itself, disappearing from view. Sander's extra soldiers hadn't arrived, leaving Leander the only one with a position on the inside. If the soldiers didn't get there before the enemy, Sander knew he and Mattias and the driver would have to take exceptional steps to avoid capture—or murder.

In the distance, Sander picked out the sound of a helicopter. He caught up to Mattias and the driver under the cover of trees.

"Stay out of sight until we know whether it's our men or--" Sander's whispers were interrupted by the vibration of his phone. He pulled it from a front pocket to glance at the screen. He'd turned off all sound so he didn't give himself away at a critical moment. Normally he shut the whole thing down, because the vibrations emitted a quiet hum that, in the dead silence of empty rooms, could be easily detected. He read the message.

Soldiers incoming.

"They're here," Sander whispered to Mattias and the driver, letting them know that shortly, the forest would come alive with movement and faint snaps of twigs.

"I'll let Leander know." Mattias pulled out his own phone and thumbed in a message.

Sander surveyed the long road leading to the entrance of the castle. Trees flanked the hard packed lane, which then opened onto a clearing. If he guessed right, Paavo—or whoever was behind this —would likely arrive by this avenue. Even if a group came at the castle from different angles, Sander figured his men had the advantage being able to scout the area and set up before the intruders arrived.

The fading chop of helicopter blades indicated Sander's soldiers had hit their drop off point and were now en route to the castle on foot.

"I'm going in through the back," Sander whispered to Mattias. "Coordinate the men out here and buzz my phone when you see anyone else on approach."

"Will do."

Parting off from Mattias and the driver, Sander followed the tree line to the back of the castle, breaking cover only when he had a straight shot to the rear entrance. He entered without the aid of a flashlight, using only the natural illumination falling in through upper windows as a guide. Deeper into the castle, where there were no windows on interior rooms, he would be forced to use his flashlight to see.

Decades of dust and other small debris made it impossible to cross the old stone floor in total silence. The open area, rising two stories, had four different hallways leading away to separate sections of the castle. Having spent time in the ruins,

Sander oriented himself in seconds. He went to the dark archway straight ahead, creeping into a cathedral shaped corridor that bypassed many parlors, strategy rooms and other living areas. In the back of his mind, he reminded himself that Leander was in here somewhere and to not let the man suddenly surprise him.

Gun clasped in both hands, Sander navigated the tomblike hallways without the aid of light, so far able to advance by feel and memory. He made it to the great halls of the entrance, with towering ceilings and rustic support beams. Lacking furniture of any kind, the enormous space provided few places to take cover. Once he was face to face with his adversary, there was no easy escape from a surprise attack. He would have to fight his way out. Windows carved high into the front walls allowed weak light to slant inside, casting milky rays onto the rugged slabs of stone.

"You make enough noise to wake the dead, old man," Leander whispered behind him.

Sander twitched at the first sound, then glanced over his shoulder. He could just make out Leander's features. Despite the light-hearted words, Leander's face was a mask of concentration and alertness. "There's a balcony up there, across from the door. I'd rather have you at my back than any other solider—just in case." Just in case his own men had somehow been compromised.

"I just came from there. It's a good vantage point. I can see this whole room and half of the staircase," Leander said, gesturing to the side, where a broad, stone staircase rose to the higher floors.

"Another sniper or two will be coming in shortly. While I set up the best positions for the flashlights, figure out where you want the extra firepower and set it up." Sander trusted Leander to arrange the soldiers in the most prime spots for defense.

"Will do." Leander pivoted away, disappearing into the dark corridor that led to the back of the castle.

Making his way to the heavy front door, Sander lifted the bracing arm and opened the door a few inches. Sharp creaks echoed off the walls from the unused, rusty hinges. He scouted the best position for a flashlight that would glow from the higher windows, visible at a distance down the long road. If this was really a meeting between king and queen, people would expect him to provide Chey a source of light. A welcoming beacon to help guide her way. Being a castle built for defense, the high windows made it difficult for enemies to gain entrance by that route, and it also made it difficult to place his flashlight where it would be seen.

He chose to angle the light against the partially open door, setting the flashlight on the floor. It was either here or up on the balcony wall.

Quiet sounds of bodies moving through the open space above indicated to Sander that his soldiers had arrived. He caught a glimpse of shadowy bodies on the balcony, then...nothing. The men found ways to blend in with the natural niches to be less visible from below.

His phone vibrated again. Sander dug it out. The message was from Mattias.

Sending a scout down the road. Everyone else in place.

Sander exhaled a slow breath. He and his men were ready.

Now all they needed was for the enemy to show its ugly head.

* * *

Sander watched the door, the staircase and the mouth of the main hallway from his crouched position against a wall. He would have rather been pacing to expend some of the energy humming through his system, except he might have made himself a target for anyone who managed to slip past the net of protection outside. Instead he put a wall at his back and got low, listening and observing for signs of life. He never heard the snipers upstairs, indicating they were hunkered down like he was.

Waiting.

He refused to consider what danger Chey might be in, refused to conjecture about her welfare or any abuse she might have already been subjected to. Thoughts of that nature would derail him quicker than anything. Instead, he contemplated different attack scenarios and his response to each. It paid to be prepared for anything.

An hour went by, and still nothing. Sander estimated the flight time between the prison and Amsler to be approximately forty minutes, yet he'd heard no sounds of a helicopter on approach. It was possible his adversary had been dropped a mile or so out and made the rest of the journey on foot. The scouts and soldiers in the woods would see any advance, he was sure.

Fifteen minutes after that, Sander stretched one leg, then the other, so he didn't develop debilitating cramps at the wrong time.

When the enemy made himself known, it wasn't by car or by foot, but from four flash-bangs thrown simultaneously at the entrances and exits of the castle. In the initial seconds, Sander pressed himself against the wall, bringing the weapon up to level toward the door. The castle itself protected him from the worst of the noise and chaos, but the men outside might now be temporarily blind and deaf.

Five, six—seven more explosions occurred. Something bounced through the crack in the front door, arching over the flashlight beam, and Sander knew instantly he had no time to make the safety of the hallway. There wasn't anywhere to hide in the great room, no furniture to duck behind. All he could do was turn away from the weapon and cover his head, hoping against hope that it wasn't a grenade. At least the flash-bang wouldn't kill him unless he was right on top of it.

Bright white light erupted across the walls, followed by a bang so loud that Sander's ears immediately started ringing. The detonation stunned him, as it was designed to do, blocking out all sounds and temporarily disabling his ability to react. Smoke slithered through the room, adding to the confusion.

A stark sense of self-preservation made Sander pivot toward the door instead of away from it, the gun leveled straight out in front of him. He coughed, eyes watering, ears ringing. The blinding sparks had fizzled out, leaving only the beam from the flashlight visible through the haze. He thought he heard someone shout, but he didn't know if it was his men, or the enemy.

The figure of a body passing by the beam of the flashlight alerted him to company; he hesitated, finger moving over the trigger. It might be the adversary —and it might be Mattias or the driver or another of his own soldiers, entering to check on his status. The haze probably blocked him from their view, too, giving him only seconds to decide what to do. This might be his only shot at a surprise of his own.

His gun fired in steady succession.

261

Booms rang through the great hall, bouncing off the walls. He tracked the motion of legs, aiming low, struggling to maintain coherency. A body fell, and another. Something ricocheted off the stone wall close to his head, the resulting crack making him go flat to the floor.

Someone was shooting back. It wouldn't be his men. They knew he was in here, waiting. Scrabbling forward, choking on the smoke, Sander belly crawled across the floor toward the place he thought the bodies went down. He didn't know if he'd shot one, two or three people. All he knew was that he was six rounds down.

Through the haze, he saw a leg, and another. The uniform pinged familiar in his memory, though it took him a second to place the navy pants with a red strip down the outside.

Russians. This was a Russian uniform.

Maybe he'd made a grave—fatal—mistake. There could be an entire army marching on Amsler, with these initial men used as scouts. He might have set an inescapable trap for himself and his men. The face that belonged to the legs wore an expression of pain and fear, mouth open as if shouting or screaming.

Sander didn't hear a thing except the ringing. He knocked the handgun out of the soldier's hand and kicked it away across the floor.

Sander saw another soldier down, and another beyond that, visible only as vague shapes until he got closer. The second guard had dropped his weapon in favor of hugging hands to his legs, two bullet wounds visible as splotches of red on the navy pants. Sander kicked that weapon away, too, and did the same to the third man. He saw the dark pant leg of a fourth victim, this one not in uniform, and had just reached the wounded man's chest when Paavo's face came into view. His brother looked startled, as if he hadn't expected to see Sander this soon. Paavo brought his arm off the floor but a boot stomped Paavo's wrist to the ground, forcing the gun out of his fingers.

Leander's voice faded in and out of Sander's hearing, shouting something he didn't understand.

Hands gripped Sander's shoulders, forcing him up and away. Sander stared at Paavo until the haze obliterated his brother from view.

Chapter Twenty

The pungent, unpleasant scent of ammonia jerked Sander into a higher state of awareness. He shot a hand out to steady his balance, and other hands gripped him in return, pushing at him until his back was firmly against the wall. Chased back by the bob of flashlight beams, the darkness parted around familiar faces: Leander, Mattias, the driver of the SUV.

"Hey, Sander. You all right, man?" Leander asked, waving the smelling salts quickly under Sander's nose.

Sander twitched away from the scent, his mental clarity clearing further. "Yeah, yeah." His ears were still ringing, just not as loud as before. "What the hell happened?"

"They lobbed flash-bangs into the courtyard, near the trees, and into the castle itself. It was a hell of a way to arrive. Me and the guys upstairs were able to get below the balcony wall in time, so we didn't get it as bad as you did," Leander said, louder than usual. Not quite shouting, but speaking above his normal tone.

"That was one approach we didn't expect," Mattias added. "We couldn't see anything and didn't dare come out of the trees in case they'd moved snipers in under the cover of smoke. That's why it took us a little while to get to you."

Sander shoved away from the wall. He noticed his gun was back in its holster, though he didn't remember putting it there. "Where is he? Did you see? Paavo's joined forces with the Russians."

"Whoa, hold on old man. Just give yourself a second to come all the way around. We've got our medic assessing the wounds of the men you shot. No one's dead, which means we'll be able to question Paavo shortly." Leander stopped Sander's progress with a firm hand on his chest.

Sander wanted to shake him off and charge into the great hall, or wherever the medic was working, to let Paavo have it. He wanted answers.

"Did you find Chey?"

"No. She's not here."

Sander pushed away from the wall

again, and this time, no one stopped him. He breathed deep, getting his bearings as he started for the sound of groans coming from a room off the long hallway. Larger, brighter flashlights spilled out the doorway, guiding him directly to the room the medic used to tend the injured. Several men were on the floor, along with Sander's own soldiers standing guard in a loose circle around them. There was no smoke here, nothing to impede Sander's view of his brother lying beside a Russian soldier. Stepping over two people, he straddled Paavo and bent down to snatch Paavo up by the collar. He lifted his brother's head three inches off the ground.

"Where is she? Are there Russian troops invading the city? Our borders? Just how far out did you sell us, Paavo?" Sander demanded. No one dared try to stop him from getting his answers.

Paavo, paler than usual due to blood loss, hair mussed out of its neat style, didn't fight Sander's hold. Two bandages wound his leg, one just above the knee, the other around his calf. His pant leg had been ripped open by the medic to get to the gunshots. Paavo said, "You should have aimed a little higher, brother."

266

"Answer the questions, Paavo. There are far worse things I can do to you besides let you rot in a jail cell. If you thought that was bad, then just keep testing me. See what else I have in store." Sander leveled his threats without hesitation. He wanted to know where his wife was, and whether his country was about to go to war.

Paavo shook with a silent laugh, but a new wariness had entered his eyes. "I have nothing to say."

One of the Russian soldiers spoke up, and it wasn't a Russian accent that fell from his lips. It was the Latvala tongue. "There are no Russian troops. He had the uniforms duplicated and--"

"Shut up, filth!" Paavo snarled.

"And what?" Leander said, hovering over the 'Russian' soldier who had decided to turn against Paavo.

"He had the uniforms duplicated and convinced us that he was in connection with the Russians—but he really wasn't. Paavo acted on his own, planned the whole thing. I'm a guard at the prison. He recruited me more than two years ago."

"Shut your mouth, or I'll have your entire family obliterated off the face of this--"

Leander cut Paavo's threat off. "No, you won't. This man might not see the outside of a jail cell for the rest of his life, but he might not get death either, and he knows if he cooperates, he's got a better shot. We'll move his family into hiding, so you can forget about sending any mercenaries."

Sander didn't look away from Paavo's face, even when Paavo diverted to snarl at the guard. His temper had the better of him. He resisted the urge to smack Paavo's head repeatedly against the cold stone floor. The more he heard from the guard, the more livid he became.

"What else? Leander asked the guard.

"The summarized version is that Paavo planned to take over Imatra so he would have a standing army. Once he had control, he meant to go to war with Latvala. He couldn't gather enough support from the citizens who had joined his cause back when Paavo tried to kill Sander, so he needed to commandeer an army of his own. Except Konstantine went to Sander for help, which *wasn't* in the plans. Paavo had his men plant the bombs both as payback, to disorient and to distract Sander and Thane, as well as throw Konstantine into a fit. He'd planned to kill Konstantine the whole time, no matter what happened. It served to throw more doubt about who was really behind the attacks."

Sander stared into Paavo's eyes as the disgusting details came forth. The amount of planning, blackmail and threats that must have occurred to make it all happen was nothing short of staggering. While Paavo had been begging to be executed or transferred to another country, he'd been plotting scenes of destruction. Planning a coup, an assassination—or two. Sander had no doubt that the death or freedom he'd denied his brother had only driven Paavo further to act.

"Where is Chey?" Sander asked in a quiet voice. The fake Russian guard, a prison guard in reality, turned his head the other way. Refusing to meet anyone's eyes.

Sander caught the action in periphery and gripped Paavo's shirt tighter in both hands. The silence in the room from all the people involved in Paavo's scheme made Sander's blood run cold. It was as if no one wanted to admit what happened to the queen.

Mattias placed a booted foot near the

injured guard's gunshot wound, threatening to create a lot more pain. "What happened to Chey?" he repeated, putting the slightest pressure just below the bandage.

The guard gasped and jerked a look at Leander, then Mattias, then Sander. He said, "She's dead. He shot her before we left the prison."

* * *

Sander, gripped in a sudden, intense rage, pulled back a fist and smashed it into Paavo's jaw. He released the shirt with his other hand and let that fist fly, too, his knuckles connecting with Paavo's jaw, his cheek. Blood erupted from Paavo's nose. Hands gripped Sander's arms and pulled him back, pulled him off, and he didn't realize he was shouting obscenities until his voice went hoarse.

Mattias stepped straight into Sander's line of sight, blocking his view of Paavo, one hand flat against Sander's chest. Three men, including Leander, held Sander back from the fallen Ahtissari prince.

"Look at me. Sander, focus. Look at me," Mattias said in a matter-of-fact voice. "Don't give him what he wants. You'll regret it for the rest of your life."

Breathing hard, fighting off bloodlust, Sander met Mattias's eyes. "I wasn't going to kill him. Only make him *wish* he was dead. He'll still wish that when I'm done with him."

"Good, good. Let's get you out of here. Leander can interrogate later. You know how good he is at that." Mattias led the way out of the room.

Sander shook off the hands that held him, sending one dark glare back to Paavo. He stepped into the hall, hands balled into fists, heart hammering in his chest. Grief threatened to consume him. He barked orders as he headed for the back exit of the castle, needing, wanting, the fresh bite of the chilly air. "Get a helicopter here. Now."

"We've got a military chopper in a clearing a quarter mile out," a guard said, somewhere behind Sander.

"Then lead the way. *Run.*"

The guard broke into a run toward the woods, holding a rifle crosswise against his body. Sander kicked into a run as well, along with Mattias and Leander and two more guards who followed close at their heels. The sweet scent of pine and the green smell of forest foliage lingered on a gentle breeze that blew through the drooping boughs. Sander fought to maintain control of himself as he ran, his knees shivering once or twice like they might give out. He had to get to Chey. Had to find her. The thought of her lying dead in the prison all this time was unthinkable.

The thought of her dead at all devastated him.

Flanked by his brother and Leander, Sander stared at nothing inside the helicopter as it lifted off and veered through the night toward the prison. He prayed for a miracle, for the guard to be wrong, for the bullet—or bullets—to have somehow missed. Maybe he would find that she'd escaped, as she was so good at doing, and on the run back to Kalev.

She couldn't be gone.

On the flight over, Mattias and Leander texted instruction to various advisors and other people of import. Plans were set in motion to find every member of Paavo's little organization and arrest them all. Interrogations would take place, with the bulk being done by Leander later, after they found Chey. Gunnar sent a message stating he was in the air with Sander's children and that Ahsan was expecting their arrival within hours.

Sander didn't want to think about having to call his kids back to tell them their mother was dead. He didn't know how he would explain, or how he would comfort them in their grief. Erick was too little to understand.

He drew in several ragged breaths and looked at the floor between his feet. He felt the light weight of Mattias's hand on his shoulder but didn't trust himself to look up. Not yet.

The second the chopper touched down, Sander jumped to the ground, weapon in hand, going in low behind Mattias. He'd ordered the helicopter to get them as close as possible. Whatever men remained of Paavo's group might not realize it wasn't Paavo returning, but the king. On the flight over, Leander had gained the numbers to the keypad on an employee gate and that was the route they took to breach the prison's perimeter. In stealth mode, the group passed one security gate after another, until they got into the building proper. Sander and Mattias both knew the general layout, having each visited the compound several times in the last few years. A guard dressed as a Russian soldier stepped out from a room into the hallway ahead of them, gun raised.

Leander took him out, the shot echoing through the corridors. Systematically, they went hall by hall, clearing rooms of hiding guards. When they rounded into the corridor containing offices and prison visitation rooms, Sander saw several dead bodies on the ground. Scattered, some wearing uniforms, others in suits. He froze, looking for feminine limbs among the more bulky, masculine shapes. The seconds stretched into agonizing eternities. Dread became a heavy weight in his chest, his throat. He didn't remember walking forward, moving through the paces as if in a dream. Blood pooled on the floor, more spattered the wall in flecks and spray patterns. The staring eyes of the dead haunted him, made his steps hesitant. He couldn't imagine looking into Chey's dead eyes. Couldn't see her stare into the veil of beyond, sightless, the vibrant lust for life snuffed out like a candle. It was too much, he couldn't breathe, couldn't think, couldn't react. He glanced past the open door of the room next to the array of bodies, and saw what he didn't want to see.

Chey on the floor. Unmoving. As still as the men at his feet. Half on her back, half on her side, a puddle of blood seeping from beneath a shoulder. He glimpsed the pale underside of her chin, the equally pale slant of her cheeks. His breath hitched.

She was dead, and his life would never be the same again.

Chapter Twenty-One

"Oh God," Mattias said, his voice just a whisper at Sander's shoulder.

Only two or three seconds had passed since Sander laid eyes on his wife, though he felt lifetimes pass under his skin, through his memories, weighing him down until his limbs felt sluggish and his breathing stuttered past his lips.

Leander bumped into him on the other side, then pushed further into the room, a chant of, *"No, no, no,"* on his lips. He sank to his knees next to Chey while shoving his gun into the shoulder holster.

Sander suddenly surged forward, sliding the gun to the blood stained table before falling into a crouch near Chey. Leander turned her over until she was flat on her back and pushed strands of dark hair away from her face.

"Chey!" Sander's grief switched to denial. He refused to accept that she could be gone. His mind raced with determination, his thoughts consumed with medical scenarios. *If she's only been dead a little while, we can bring her back. We can do CPR and she'll come around. We just need to get her breathing, need to get her heart started.*

Leander pressed two fingers against the pulse in Chey's throat. "...she's alive. I can feel a pulse—it's faint—but it's there. She's alive."

Sander, just about to start CPR, snapped a look at Leander. "Are you sure? She looks--"

"I know," Leander said, apparently commiserating with the fact that Chey had looked dead. *Did* look dead. With her pale skin and stillness. "She's barely hanging on. We need to evacuate her to a hospital. Right now."

"I'm on with our private doctors right now. They're expecting her," Mattias said from the doorway. He had his phone to his ear, speaking quickly to someone on the other line.

Sander chided himself for not thinking to check her pulse in the seconds when he'd dropped to his knees. He blamed his inability to think straight on shock. Not about to waste any more time, he gathered Chey in his arms and pressed to a stand.

Leander retrieved his gun and followed him to the door.

Mattias took the lead out of the prison, weapon up and ready. They had encountered everyone left alive; if there were other officers or more of Paavo's guards, they were in hiding.

"Stay with me," Sander whispered to Chey. "The kids need you. I need you. Please, please don't leave me." She felt so limp in his arms. He feared she might stop breathing any second, and dipped his head down to listen as he stepped over bodies, his pace quick in Mattias's wake. Once they were outside in the chilly night, he navigated the gate system with Leander and Mattias's help, cursing silently at the delay every time Leander had to punch in numbers.

Then they were running across the open space to the helicopter, Sander doing his best not to jostle his wife. He stepped up into the craft and cradled Chey across his lap, her blood smearing his shirt, his pants, his arms.

Mattias made a quick phone call as everyone strapped in. He directed military captains to the prison to lock it down and take back control from any lingering combatants. It needed to be done sooner than later.

Leander sat next to Sander, feeling for Chey's pulse every few minutes as the chopper got in the air.

Staring down at Chey's face, her lashes dusky crescents on alabaster cheeks, Sander willed her to live. He also apologized profusely, in silence, for letting her down. He'd missed critical clues somewhere, should have known his brother was ultimately behind the attacks. If he would have sent her and the children off sooner, this wouldn't have happened.

He recognized his stages of grief even as he passed through them. Caught between regret and apology, Sander promised that if she would just pull through, if she would live, that he would do everything different. He would protect her better, be more aware of the dangers living this life entailed. After the devastation last time, he'd gone to extreme lengths to protect his family, but it just wasn't enough.

Maybe, he admitted to himself, it would never be enough.

He smoothed his fingers through her hair at the temple, then leaned down to press his lips against her forehead. Her

279

skin felt cooler than normal. It sent a fresh spike of fear through him and he checked her pulse.

So very faint.

"Stay with me," he repeated. "We're almost there. The doctors will have you fixed up in no time. Do you hear me? Just a few more minutes, Chey. Hang in there."

Sander kissed her brow again, and again. He smoothed the back of his knuckles across her cheekbone, scared out of his mind that this would be the last time he got to show her affection. Got to hold her while she still breathed.

The chopper touched down on the rooftop of Kalev hospital some time later, an agonizing amount of time as far as Sander was concerned. He climbed down and laid Chey on a waiting gurney, the wind from the helicopter blades blowing his hair every which way. The doctors and nurses hustled the gurney away from the helipad toward the rooftop elevator, their scrubs rustling, surgical gowns flapping against their legs.

It was a race against time, and time was not on their side.

* * *

Sander's final glimpse of Chey was one of orderly chaos and sweet poignancy. While doctors and nurses scrambled to save her, Chey lay passive and helpless, her face nearly cherubic with youth and innocence. Sander watched the gurney disappear through swinging doors, the doctors promising to update him as soon as possible.

He slid his hands in his pockets, staring but not seeing, all the adrenaline in his system evaporating in an instant. His shoulders sagged and his spine felt heavy. He knew he had things to do, that he should get on the phone with advisors and councilmen and military commanders.

Sander couldn't bring himself to move, not one inch, much less concentrate on business.

Mattias and Leander stood next to him, glancing at the door and then his face. Sander knew it, could see their concern in periphery, but didn't acknowledge their silent questions.

No, he wasn't all right. No, he didn't want to sit down. No, he didn't want a drink. He wanted—he wanted happiness back. He wanted to see Chey trot down the long stairs at Kallaster castle, energetic and lively, with the girlish smile she reserved just for him. He wanted to play with his children in the sand, with the sun shining down, while Chey heckled him from the sidelines. Long dates, slow nights of passion, adventures to other countries, kicking back on the balcony. There was so much left to do.

Seven years was not long enough with the love of his life.

He needed forever.

* * *

Over the next three hours, the hospital filled with friends and family. Sander wouldn't leave those closest to Chey, who loved her as much as he did, in the dark about the seriousness of her condition. He refused to move too far away from the doors they'd wheeled Chey through, pacing near the wall as other doctors and nurses came and went. The friends and family who came to see him, to give him words of hope and optimism, understood his desire to remain separate from the growing legion of visitors in the special waiting area set aside for royalty. He needed to be alone, to pace and figure out his emotions.

Sander wanted to be the first to learn whether Chey lived or died.

There were tears and flowers, prayers and vigils, and the occasional presence of Mattias and Leander. They flitted in and out of his periphery like ghosts, checking on him, bringing him water. With security at an all time high around the hospital, Mattias and Leander were afforded the time to be near Sander. To be near family and friends.

Leander's wife, Wynn, was inconsolable. Chey's best friend since childhood, the two girls were all but inseparable. Wynn took the news harder than anyone but Sander.

Mattias handed his cell phone off to Sander at one point, and said, "I've been on the line with Gunnar. They're on the way back. Elias wants to talk to you."

Bracing himself, Sander put the phone to his ear. He knew Gunnar hadn't told the kids what was going on, only that they needed to get back to Latvala. There wasn't any need to scare the kids when they were still hours away from landing.

"Papa! We're not going to get to see Uncle Ahsan after all," Elias said.

It almost broke Sander to hear his

son's voice. He swallowed several times. "I know, I'm sorry, son. Soon though. We'll...we'll all go for a visit. How's that?"

"All right! Me and Em and Erick and you and mom can all ride horses in the desert!"

Sander leaned his back against a wall and tipped a look at the ceiling. He could feel Mattias's searching stare. It took great effort to smooth the tremble from his voice. He said, "Yes, we can. I'm sure Uncle Ahsan won't mind. Listen Elias, I have to go. We'll see you in a few hours."

"Dad?"

"Yes?"

"Are you okay?"

Sander's chest seized. He breathed through the next few seconds. Leave it to his astute son to pick up on the fact that he didn't sound like himself, no matter how hard he was trying to be 'normal'. Kids knew. They always knew.

"Yeah. I'm all right. There's a lot going on right now, son. That's all. I love you."

"Love you, papa!"

Sander ended the call and handed the phone back to Mattias. "Just hold all calls for now."

"Do you need anything else?" Mattias asked, sliding the phone into his pocket.

"Not right now, thanks." If he was honest, just having his brother at his side was a balm against the storm of his emotions. It seemed Mattias knew, because he leaned against the wall, too, falling into silence. Waiting, simply being a companion in a time of trouble.

When the surgery doors opened and the doctors strode through, Sander straightened, darting looks between their neutral faces, desperate to know the news. And yet deathly afraid they would shake their heads, negating all his hopes and dreams.

"It was close," one doctor said, snagging the cap off his head. He had silver at the temples of his blonde hair and a golden complexion that suggested he had recently returned from a long vacation in sunnier climes.

"She lost a lot of blood," the second doctor added. He was darker, with hazel eyes that met Sander's in a forthright manner. "But she pulled through the surgery and we're expecting a full recovery. She'll need to remain here for another several days until she's out of danger."

"Thank God," Sander whispered. His relief was temporarily overwhelming.

"Thank you. When can I see her?" He shook each of the doctor's hands.

"She's in recovery now, your Majesty. She's not awake, but you're welcome to sit with her."

Sander inclined his head and said to Mattias, "Tell the others, will you? I'm going in."

"I will. I'm very happy to hear she'll pull through." Mattias's own relief was obvious and sincere. He pulled Sander into a brief but warm hug.

Sander embraced Mattias tightly, sharing a moment of emotion together, before he stepped away. He had a recovering wife to see.

Chapter Twenty-Two

Beeps and clicks. Shuffles of clothing. A tingle on her arm. Whooshes and sighs. Chey heard the sounds from a distance. She didn't know what it meant, or why everything seemed to be on repeat.

Beeps and clicks. Whooshes and sighs. Shuffles of clothing.

She tried to open her eyes, slow to shrug off the sluggishness that plagued her. Everything beyond her lashes was a blur of gray and white, the shapes indistinguishable from one another.

Why couldn't she wake up?

A darker shadow blocked out the gray and white, looming above her head. She couldn't make out details. This time, a different sound combined with the rest; a rumbling groan that she realized, after a moment, came from herself.

Instantly, a pleasant baritone—a familiar baritone—obliterated all the other noises.

"Chey? Chey, can you hear me?"

Sander. Now she recognized the shape of his head, the beloved features as her vision started to clear. "Where am I?" She wasn't sure why he peered down at her like that, eyes suspiciously watery—or perhaps that was just her imagination.

"You're in the hospital. Recovering from surgery."

Beeps and clicks. Shuffles of clothing. Tubes and wires. Whooshes and sighs.

"Oh," she said, more breath than sound. She couldn't feel much below the neck, though she did feel Sander's warm hand around her own. Images rushed back as she studied his face, the concern in his eyes switching to affection and adoration. She whispered, "Paavo shot me."

Sander licked his lips. Fury flickered in and out of his gaze. "He said he did, yes. But how are you feeling? Are you in pain? Should I get the doctor?"

"No doctor." Chey didn't want anything to disturb her time with Sander. She needed to tell him how serious the situation was with Paavo. "He's got the prison. Sander, he means to come after you--"

"Shh, shh. I know. We've got him in custody and are rounding up his men.

Don't worry, we've got it under control. You just concentrate on healing and getting better." He stroked the back of his fingers gently across her cheek.

Chey realized that Sander was suffering greatly. She could feel the waves of angst and worry, could read the desperation in his features. There was relief, too. "I'll be okay. I don't feel too bad, really." Probably because she couldn't feel most of her body. Drugs, she thought, and left over anesthesia from surgery. The pain would come, she knew, as the narcotics wore off.

"I don't imagine you do. You're slurring as bad as a drunk sailor," he said.

Chey laughed, or thought she laughed. A sound burbled in her throat, a faint echo of her usual boisterous belly laughs.

Sander bent down to brush several kisses to her forehead. He whispered against her skin. "I love you more than anything. Thank you for staying."

It was only then that she realized she must have had a closer call than she thought. Had she almost died? Chey remembered the gun going off, a blossom of pain, and falling. She remembered the shock of *knowing* she'd been shot—and then nothing.

"I love you, too," she whispered back. "I'm sorry if I gave you a scare." Chey recalled how frightened she'd been when Sander sank into a coma after an attack on his caravan.

He leaned back far enough to see her eyes. "It wasn't your fault. You didn't know he'd pull a gun on you."

"But I shouldn't have ever gone to the prison. I should have stayed home--" Chey gasped, her whole body twitching when she thought of the kids. "Sander, where are the kids? You have to--"

"Don't worry, don't worry. They were on their way to Ahsan's but now they're flying home. They should be here in an hour or so. They're fine, they're all right," he reassured her.

Pain lanced through her chest and shoulder and down into her right arm. The numbness from anesthesia was starting to wear off. That was the only reason she felt the tension ease in her limbs and torso. "You're sure they'll be safe? Maybe you should have let them go to Afshar." Against her will, her lashes closed. She pried them open.

"I told them we'll all go for a short vacation. Ahsan will love the company. He and everyone else has sent you well wishes and lots of love, too. They're in the waiting room with about a thousand bouquets and tons of chocolate." He smoothed a hand over her hair, a light but endearing touch.

"All right." She suddenly didn't have the energy to say all the things she wanted to say. Her lashes drooped again. "Sander?"

"Yes? I'm here." He gently squeezed her fingers.

"Please don't leave. Don't leave when I go to sleep." She couldn't stay awake any longer. Darkness was dragging her down, down...

* * *

The next time Chey opened her eyes, she had less trouble focusing. It didn't take as long for her to bring all the smiling, crying faces into view. The clicks and beeps were ever present, along with the whoosh-sigh of the electric door. She saw Sander, who had apparently honored her wish to remain at her side, standing next to the bedside with one hand on her arm. He wore the same dark clothes and his whiskers looked a little more prominent. Wynn, her best friend, sobbed a hello and kissed Chey's temple.

"We were so worried. Thank God you're all right," Wynn said.

Chey didn't have time to give specific thank-yous. More people moved in to the side of the bed opposite Sander, spending just a second on hellos and well wishes. Leander, Mattias, Mattias's girlfriend Alannah, Natalia, Krislin...Gunnar's wife, and several of Sander's cousins cycled through, touching her arm and her hand or leaving whispery kisses on her cheek. She murmured her thanks for their visit as the group filed out again. In their wake, the gray and white room had been transformed with hundreds of flowers. Vases sat on tables lining the wall, filled to the brim with every kind of flower known to man. It was an explosion of color that brought cheer to the room.

"How're you feeling?" Sander asked, squeezing her hand. His palm smoothed up and down her forearm, a light touch that didn't disturb the wires and tubes.

"Rough," she admitted. "But all right. You look like you could use some sleep."

He smiled, the corners of his eyes crinkling. Bending down, he kissed her cheek. "I'll sleep later. Right now, there are a few other people who are desperate to see you."

Sander glanced over his shoulder.

Chey released a little sound of excitement when Elias ran into the room. He looked more and more like Sander every day. She held out her other arm, inviting her oldest son—and the heir to the Latvala throne—into her embrace. Elias hugged himself to her side, blue eyes worried yet curious. Emily ran in next, shouting for her mother, dark hair pulled back into a ponytail. She wore an adorable white dress with pink piping along the hem and around the collar. Sander lifted the little girl to sit opposite Elias, cautioning her in a quiet voice to be gentle. Emily leaned in and laid her head on Chey's stomach, one tiny hand petting Chey's arm.

Overwhelmed to see the kids, Chey cooed and reassured them that she was fine. Mattias returned with Erick in tow. The youngest prince let out a squeal when he saw Chey, then silenced his excitement as he took in the medical equipment.

She accepted him into the curl of her arm and whispered against his forehead, asking if he'd been a good boy and if he'd enjoyed the plane ride. There was no better feeling than to have her children nestled close. She met Sander's eyes, noting the gleam there while he stroked his hand over Erick's head, hovering at the baby's side so he didn't fall off the bed. Ever protective.

Chey fielded the children's questions as best she could, leaving out any specific details. Elias, proving to be as astute as his father, queried whether she would be able to use her arm, the one in the sling, to play catch on the sand. Every weekend, their little family unit spent time at the shore, letting the kids play and build sandcastles. Elias didn't want anything to do with such mundane tasks; he liked to play catch with a football and engage Sander in mock sword fights. She said that yes, eventually, she would be right back out there with the rest of them, intercepting the ball as usual. Elias delighted in Chey's flare of mischief.

After fifteen minutes of company, Sander began the tedious task of separating the kids from Chey. Kisses were passed out and goodbyes echoed through the room. She watched the kids go with relief and longing. Relief that she was still alive to see them grow into maturity, and longing not to miss out on too much while she recovered. She was a prominent part of their every day lives, preferring to do the majority of the work involved in raising a family.

"I know you're going to have to go back to Pallan island sooner than later to deal with all this," Chey said once the electric door whooshed closed.

Sander stood next to the side of the bed. He might have been tired, but he also looked determined.

"Mattias is taking care of some of it for me. He's doing press conferences and dealing with the advisors. I've been making a few calls while you were asleep, too. Tomorrow, there is a council meeting about my brother and the consequences of his actions. I should probably attend. Imatra has been thrown into chaos with the death of Konstantine, and I'm hearing Aleksi, the heir to the throne, has requested a meeting with me. I can probably fit that in after the council meeting."

"I never did get to tell you all of Paavo's confessions. Some of it might have a bearing on your decisions in your meetings." She smoothed her fingertips over the back of Sander's knuckles.

"Did he tell you his whole plan?"

"Mostly. The basics of it. I definitely don't understand where he's at in his head, but then, no one does. He said that part of the attack was payback, and part to distract Latvala and Somero while he made a play for Imatra. He wanted their army so he could attack you. Konstantine, he pointed out, had been slated to die all along. And I think the only reason he didn't get you was because I intercepted his calls to see you and went in your stead. He would have gotten the jump on you at the prison, since he'd done such a good job of throwing suspicion onto the Russians. I think he was angry that you let him stew in prison as long as you did. He hates it. And he's very vengeful. He wants you to pay, and pay big, for denying him either death or exile." She paused, then added, "He threatened the kids. Told me that if I didn't tell him where you were, that he'd take them out one by one."

A hard expression crossed Sander's face. Turning away from the bed, he put his hands on his hips and stared at the floor.

Chey knew he was fighting against the urge to go rearrange Paavo's face. Or worse. Sander was not a cold blooded killer, but he would find a way to make his bother pay for daring to involve children in his scheme.

"You know. Members of the council are calling for his execution. They know he'll be found guilty in court, and they want to end his life." Sander spoke in a quiet voice. "I've always resisted, because...he *is* my brother, and I don't think I could watch him die. But he's unhinged and dangerous, and if I let him live, he'll try again. And again. He'll compromise guards, send notes through blackmailed officers, and wreak havoc on our lives. To think he might actually harm one of my children makes me livid. To know he tried to kill you, and nearly succeeded, tempts me to go against the moral code I've lived by all my life and strangle him in his cell. It tempts me, but ultimately, he wins if he brings me down that far. He wins, and I'll have to suffer the rest of my life with my bad decision. Paavo knows it, too, which is why I'm sure he's gloating at the position he's put me in. I've considered whether the court deciding to put him to death will shift the burden of guilt I know I'll feel, but I don't think it will. The best way to make Paavo suffer for what he's done is to put him right back where he doesn't want to be—in prison. Except things will have to change so he can't compromise any more men...or blackmail them. I'm willing to go to an extreme in that regard, since I can't kill him."

Chey shifted in the hospital bed, one hand gripping the guard rail. She watched Sander's back as he talked, listened to the subtle changes in his voice when he spoke of death, of guilt, and of ultimate retribution. As upset and angry as she was over Paavo pulling the trigger on her, and threatening her children, she was still glad to know that Sander intended to take the high road instead of sinking into the skin of a murderer. He was a better man for controlling his baser urges. She also knew what a toll the entire situation was taking on him. Sander wasn't a man, or a king, who made decisions lightly. He took everything to heart; any missteps would haunt him for years.

"You're doing the right thing. Sending him back to prison—or some kind of confinement, is what he fears most. Even more than death. I agree that you should make changes in how you deal with anyone in charge of his care. Although is there anyone who can't be blackmailed, anyone who can't be bought for a price? I'm not sure."

Sander's shoulders lifted and settled with his next deep breath. "I'll just have to take out anyone's ability to communicate with him."

Chey's brow flickered with curiosity. She didn't see how that was possible. Someone had to give Paavo food every day, had to deliver toiletries and give the man access to a shower. Sander had something on his mind, however, and only time would tell what it was.

"Sander."

He hesitated, then turned a brooding look over his shoulder.

Chey held his gaze. "We won't underestimate him again. No one could have foreseen that he would go to such lengths. That he had the means to blackmail guards and rally support from the people who stood behind him the first time. I know you'll make the best decision for everyone involved. You do what you have to." Whatever kind of retribution he could live with.

He inclined his head. Backtracking to the bed, he bent down to kiss her on the mouth. Whispering against her lips, he said, "I don't know what I'd do without you, Chey Ahtissari."

Chapter Twenty-Three

At two-minutes til noon the next day, Sander stepped into the meeting chamber at Kallaster castle where Paavo's fate would be decided. He already knew what he was going to say, no matter what the verdict would be. Attired in a sharp suit of black with a black vest and white shirt, he crossed to a chair separate from the rows of tiered seating housing the councilmen. There were at least fifty men present. Each stood with a show of respect and deference, inclined their heads, then reclaimed their seats. The chamber, with its ornate, carved wood walls and somber atmosphere, was a different venue than the usual room the men gathered in for their decisions about the welfare of Latvala. Here, with the spartan furnishings, plain stone floor, and minimal lighting, harder decisions were voted upon regarding intimate royal affairs.

A hush fell over the room as he sat.

Sander felt every eye upon him. Stretching out his legs, he rested his arms on the sides of the chair and glanced at the councilmen. Some had served since his father's era, fewer were new additions. Urmas, a folder in his hands, paced between the rows of seating and Sander's chair but paused to add a bow of his head.

Sander didn't waste time. He opened at the heart of the matter. "As you all know, prince Paavo and several others are in custody for plotting to precipitate war between Imatra and Latvala, as well as murder, *attempted* murder and treason. I've decided to allow the council to decide the fate of the men involved in Paavo's scheme. I want investigations done to find out if the guards were supporters before, blackmailed recently, or something different. I want answers. As far as prince Paavo, I want a show of hands to see who votes for life in prison."

Not one councilman raised his hand. The majority wanted death, which would make Sander's order that much harder for the bloodthirsty council to accept.

"Execution?"

Hands went up across the board. Urmas made notes in the folder as the verdict came down.

"After much consideration, knowing what I know about my brother's intentions, desires and fears, I've decided to overrule the council. Paavo will be sent to Macor."

A rush of whispers and gasps swept through the room.

"But your majesty--"

"That's *hardly* punishment--"

"Sending him to a *castle,* your Majesty?"

"Hear me out," Sander said, cutting off the protests. He knew what they were going to say. "As you all know, Macor is an Ahtissari stronghold—a ruin—in the hinterlands. It's a smaller fortress once used by guards to watch for advances from our eastern border. There are two floors and five large rooms, plus a living area, kitchen area and several bathrooms. The fortress was stripped of all furniture and hardware decades ago. There is no basement or dungeon or other secretive passages in or out. Its location well away from populated areas serves my purpose well. Four outbuildings exist around the premises. I've decided to have Paavo live out his term at the fortress instead of the prison."

Another flash of whispers and startled noises echoed through the chamber. Sander continued before any councilmen could voice their objections.

"The lower level windows will be sealed with iron bars, as well as the upper floor, providing no escape. A specific team of my own choosing will reside in the outer buildings in shifts, men whose loyalty I trust. They'll provide meals and other minor necessities—toilet paper, shampoo, soap—and keep watch over the fortress through remote security feeds that allow minimal interaction between the guards and my brother. Paavo will be stripped of all entertainment, access to humanity, and other stimulation. You may find this cruel—I find it fitting. And necessary."

One councilman stood, cheeks ruddy with indignation. "Your Majesty, excuse my bluntness--"

"That's never stopped you before, Heinlam," Sander pointed out. A few chuckles swept through the council.

"No, it has not. And it will serve us well here today," Heinlam continued with a grunt. "The council has spoken in depth on this issue. We collectively feel it is far too risky to allow the prince to live. He has attempted a coup before—now he's

304

escalated to war. He irreparably damaged Ahtissari castle, nearly murdered the queen, and is accountable for hundreds of innocent deaths. The people of Latvala have had their resolve shaken again, and that's not what will help us going forward to heal this country. We have heard from King Aleksi, now on the throne after his brother Konstantine's death, and from King Thane. Each has requested the highest possible punishment—death, your Majesty—for the attacks on their countries. Otherwise, their ambassadors have suggested Imatra and Somero will fight to have prince Paavo tried on their own soil, and the verdict will be the same. Everyone but you, it seems, believes the penalty of death is the *only* answer here."

The chamber fell to complete silence. A thorough silence, the same kind of stillness found in tombs.

Sander studied the speaker, then the council. He made eye contact with a dozen men while he considered the appeal. As he knew they would, the members had made a compelling case. To know that the Kings of Imatra and Somero suggested they would try Paavo on their own soil for his crimes didn't surprise him—that was standard protocol. Aleksi really had no other choice. His country, although in turmoil when Konstantine ruled, was facing the same upheaval Latvala faced after Paavo's attempted coup. Despite all that, Sander did not feel the same. He stood by his decision.

"I hear and recognize your concerns. I have a meeting later today with Aleksi as you know, and I'll meet with Thane tomorrow. We'll work out the differences between us. As far as Paavo—my decision remains." Sander paused when more councilmen got to their feet in protest. He waited out the initial blustering and indignation. Finally, when his silence forced the councilmen to quiet down, Sander rose from his chair. Sliding his hands into his pockets, he paced before the ascending rows of councilmen. "Execution may appear to be the only solution to suit Paavo's crimes, but I believe we are giving him exactly what he wants—other than exile—if we do that. He has repeatedly begged me to be executed or exiled. Paavo understands exile is a near impossibility, so death, in his estimation, is the only recourse. *That* is the depth of his discontent at being forced to live his life out in a cell. To pay me back for keeping him locked up these last years, he managed to plot the chaos that we see around us. Desperation of that caliber knows no bounds. I, for one, am not willing to give Paavo what he wants. Freedom with exile, or freedom with death. He will live out his life at Macor, knowing that every day will be like the day before, that this time, there will be no escape. No master plot toward the ruin of *any* country. For those who think this will happen again, I can assure you, it will not. The steps I'm taking are sufficient to disconnect Paavo from the rest of the world forever."

"We thought he was contained this time, too, in prison," Heinlam said, talking over the chorus of discussion rampaging through the council.

"Prison has all the standard safety precautions. No one has ever escaped any of our prisons, so it's not the security itself that's the problem. Weak minded men, men subjected to blackmail—that was the problem. I've corrected this at Macor, and will also be overhauling our prison personnel so that blackmail and death threats against officers will be less effective."

Heinlam turned to his fellow council

members. Quick discourse took place, the men gesturing with their hands, some openly angry, others conflicted.

Sander waited out the uproar. This was a part of their process, how the upper council and the king came to hard decisions. The arguments for and against the final verdict—already settled in Sander's mind—would happen here. Now. The councilmen deserved time to appeal and to express their discontent or support.

After fifteen minutes of hard discourse, Heinlam bellowed a new vote. "Those in support of Macor?"

Eight men raised their hands.

"As you can see, your Majesty, we are far apart on the vote. Simply—the council strongly disagrees with your decision," Heinlam said to Sander.

"I have eyes," Sander said, even though he knew Heinlam was following protocol by garnering another vote. "As before, I understand your position," Sander said to the council at large. "In this particular case, I choose to overrule the majority and follow through with my decision."

"The citizens of Latvala will never forgive you if Paavo gets loose again, or orchestrates another attack on the country from his new 'prison'," Heinlam warned.

Sander paced the same languid figure eight across the floor. "When history looks back on my reign, on my legacy, what will it say? Will it say I was a fair, just leader? Or will it say I was the king who put his brother to death? Words on paper will never capture the emotion of *this* moment, gentlemen. Text cannot capture the angst of our losses, the grief of those directly related to the bombings, or the intensity of deciding whether a man lives or dies. The stories of the future will boil down to the base details: Sander sent his brother, the bomber, the murderer, to death. Nowhere will it state my personal reasons for or against that verdict. People will see what's on the surface. There is no doubt whatsoever that Paavo deserves punishment. No one disputes that. But I would rather my legacy show that I acted with humanity in the face of overwhelming diversity. That is by far *not* the sole reason for my decision, but I recognize it will be remembered long after my bones turn to dust. In my opinion, this is the best punishment to fit the crime, even above death." He paused to take in the measure of his council. Then, he added, "It is my final decision. See it done."

The council members stood and bowed their heads, acknowledging Sander's order.

Departing the chamber, Sander stalked the halls of Kallaster, desperate to clear his mind of the council meeting before his session with the new king of Imatra. Sander braced himself for yet another person to insist he send his brother to death.

* * *

By the time Sander opened the door to the formal parlor, he had himself under better control. He'd spent the time between the council meeting and now pacing the grotto, thinking about what to say to Aleksi should the new king demand a different justice than the one Sander had already ordered for Paavo. It was a delicate situation, and Sander was honestly grieved that his own flesh and blood had assassinated the ruling king of a neighboring country. He'd also done a bit of homework the night before, sitting by Chey's bedside. Sander had learned that Aleksi, one of four surviving siblings to Konstantine, was but twenty-four years old, was a member of the Imatra military, and a man exceedingly skilled at self defense. He'd discovered by not so public means that Aleksi was versed in martial arts, swordplay, weaponry, and excelled at traversing complicated outdoor obstacle courses. Aleksi wasn't a man to sit idle in his downtime from whatever duties he executed as a former prince. Now he was king, and judging by the texts sent from Leander, Sander figured Aleksi to be a formidable ruler.

His first sighting of the new king backed up Sander's initial suppositions. Aleksi paced near the fireplace, hands in his pockets, a thoughtful look on his face. Olive skinned, with angular features and light brown hair worn loose around his head, king Aleksi looked as honed as Sander expected him to be. The king was shorter than his own six-foot-three frame by maybe an inch, no more than two. The sharp suit of black fit him well.

Aleksi glanced up as the door opened, then diverted his steps to meet Sander halfway. The formal parlor was dressed in luxurious furnishings, with a tall fireplace and family portraits lining the walls. It resembled other formal sitting areas and parlors throughout Kallaster castle.

"King Ahtissari, thank you for meeting me," Aleksi said, extending his hand.

Sander grasped it and shook. "Thank you for coming. May I first extend my sincere apologies for what happened to Konstantine."

"Thank you." Aleksi withdrew his hand. "And please, call me Aleksi."

"Sander." He gestured to the seating arrangement, which had been specifically placed for the men to face each other without being awkward. "Please, sit. Can I get you anything before we start?"

"Your service has been excellent so far, Sander. I already have coffee." Aleksi gestured to an end table where a steaming mug waited.

Sitting across from Aleksi, Sander noted the drink with a satisfied nod. "All right. I would ask what brings you to Latvala, but I'm sure it's unnecessary."

Aleksi unbuttoned his coat and flipped an end aside before he sat down. Instead of leaning back, he sat on the edge of the cushion, torso tilted forward. Sander took that as a sign of agitation. Restlessness. As had the pacing. He knew, because he did it all the time himself.

"It has been a shocking week, ending with the assassination of my brother and my sudden ascension to the throne. I wanted to speak with you face to face, Sander, because I wanted to apologize for the situation my brother put you in. I became aware of his 'offer', or his demands, after he had been here to see you. Should I have known before that, I would have done everything in my power to stop him," Aleksi said.

Surprised, Sander listened and observed as Aleksi proceeded to apologize rather than demand Paavo's head on a platter. There was still time, he reminded himself. "I will admit his...suggestion did not sit all that well with me."

Aleksi rubbed a thumb into the middle of his opposite palm. "I discerned as much from Konstantine's ranting after returning to Imatra. I want you to know that just because of our father's history, and Konstantine's unstable rule as king--"

"Wait, excuse my interruption, Aleksi. What did you mean, our father's history?" Sander frowned; as far as he knew, the two kings hadn't ever agreed on any formal alliance, and thus, Aksel had shunned Konstantine's father, leaving a gap between the two countries. Sander had grown up never hearing much about Imatra other than there were better countries to align with.

Aleksi looked surprised in turn. "You were never told about their battles? Between him and my father? Years past, they attempted several alliances, all of which failed because the men didn't get along. Aksel and Alder were at each other's throats from the beginning, so I'm told. I never did quite understand what set them off, only that father would come storming home from another meeting with Aksel, frustrated that they could not come to equal terms. It ended in a permanent separation, where the men wouldn't even talk."

This was news to Sander. Aksel had rarely said anything regarding Imatra to Sander, and never in harsh terms. Aksel had been dismissive and blasé about the country, writing them off as possible allies early on. "Interesting. My father never mentioned much about Imatra at all, actually. I guess that's why we have no accord, no trade agreements and no alliance. I don't recall him ever even mentioning Alder by name."

Aleksi's brows arched at the news.

"That's interesting. Anyway, I'm here because I don't want my brother's actions to cause a rift between our countries."

"If you don't mind my saying—you don't seem upset at Konstantine's assassination." Sander couldn't detect a lot of emotion from Aleksi, but he might have been the type of man to hide it well, especially in formal meetings with foreign heads of state. "I don't judge a man by someone else's actions, only his own."

Aleksi paused, hesitating just long enough to make Sander think the king was trying to decide how much to divulge.

"In truth, Sander, Konstantine and I did not get along well at all. Many thought Konstantine too unstable to even take the throne, but he ascended and threw the country into turmoil, as I'm sure you heard. I'm trying to rectify some of that. I'm saddened that he's dead—he *is* my flesh and blood. Even as a child he was distant from the rest of us, always off learning how to become king. I suspect it wasn't his fault, exactly."

"Mm. I have a brother I am at odds with as well. I'm sure you've heard," Sander said in an unamused tone. There was no use hiding the ill will between Paavo and Sander. The whole world knew that Paavo had attempted a coup, and now he'd bombed three separate countries.

"It's no secret," Aleksi admitted.

"We'll have our people talk over a fair restitution for the damage and loss to Imatra--"

Aleksi held up a hand in a stop motion. "There's no need, Sander. I didn't come here to demand money. Konstantine lied to you about those skirmishes and could have sent your country to war ahead of the problems Paavo was perpetrating. I'd say we're even. Which is why I'd like to start fresh between us, perhaps leave future trade deals open for discussion."

Sander inclined his head, easily accepting Aleksi's offer. "I'm definitely open to discussion. By the way—Paavo won't be put to death. He'll be transferred to a distant location, the only prisoner on the premises, and will live out the rest of his life there. I want you to know before it hits the media."

Aleksi studied Sander with an intent, serious expression. "My advisors insisted that I request death, but that is an acceptable punishment. You're sure he won't be able to bring up an army from there?"

"No. His interaction with humans in general will be almost nonexistent. Trust me when I say relegating Paavo to a life in a secular prison will be the best punishment anyone can give him. Death would be preferable, as Paavo told me so many times. I refuse to give him what he really wants besides exile." Behind closed doors, in an official yet private conversation, Sander didn't hesitate to be honest with Aleksi. These were the times when strong bonds formed between leaders of countries—or at least generated enough trust for the countries to work well together.

"I understand." Aleksi inclined his head. "I know you must have a great deal to do. Thank you for seeing me on short notice."

Sander stood from the chair and extended his hand. He thought Aleksi would make a far better king than Konstantine. "Thank you for coming. I look forward to more meetings in the near future, Aleksi."

"As do I." Aleksi stepped toward the door.

Sander followed Aleksi into the hall. While the new king of Imatra departed for his homeland, Sander began preparations for sending Paavo to Macor.

He intended to escort his brother to the stronghold himself to say one final goodbye.

Chapter Twenty-Four

The next two days were busy days for Sander. He met with Thane, visited the slowly recovering Chey, attended his children, and ordered the necessary changes to Macor. The council members had appealed his decision in an emergency meeting that did not change Sander's mind about the outcome of Paavo's fate. He was set on a course of action and meant to see it through.

Mattias, Leander and Gunnar all played important roles in picking up the slack regarding the destruction at Ahtissari castle and fielding interviews with the media. The citizens needed reassurance and answers, which Mattias provided in his stoic, serious demeanor.

On the third day, Sander escorted Chey home from the hospital. He breathed easier when they arrived at Kallaster castle, which was still under heightened security after the attacks, and guided Chey with an arm around her waist toward the stairs to their suite. Most of the castle staff applauded Chey's return, many bearing flowers and little gifts, some with smiles, others with tears. Chey had earned—and deserved—the love and respect so clearly aimed her way. She had proven to be caring, compassionate, fiercely protective of Latvala's citizens and loyal to her duties as queen. Her penchant for calling people by name and taking a more laid-back approach to rule made her personable and well liked.

"I can carry you up the stairs," Sander said near her ear. He worried it might be too much too soon. The doctors had released Chey with the agreement that she wouldn't overdo it. Sander knew Chey, however. He knew the depths of her determination and stubbornness.

"I can do it," she said, using her good hand to grasp the banister. She ascended with more energy in her step than Sander could believe.

He hovered close anyway, half tempted to carry her the rest of the way because he *wanted* to. Instead, he respected her will to do it for herself, understanding without being told that she needed the sense of accomplishment.

"Last one to the top is a rotten egg," he

teased, earning a laugh from Chey.

"You'd fall over if I started jogging up these stairs," Chey said, throwing him a teasing glance.

"You start jogging and I really *will* carry you. And ground you."

She scoffed. At the second landing, she paused to get her breath. Chey could run these stairs several times over with no problem; that she was a little winded proved to Sander that she indeed had more recovery time ahead. Without asking, he scooped her up in his arms and carried her the rest of the way.

"I don't want to hear any complaining. You want to feel accomplished, I get it, but I'm relieved you're home and am happy to carry you to our room." If luck had been any less on their side, Sander might have been returning a widower. The thought made him shudder.

"You have no idea how happy I am to be here, too. The people at the hospital are great, but there really is no place like home. The food is better, the company is better...and look, my bed." Chey cooed when Sander toted her across the threshold to their suite and into the bedchamber, where the king sized bed waited. He rumbled a laugh, sending another silent thank-you into the ether for her safety.

His life would have never been the same without her.

As he set her gently on the bed, she curled a hand around his nape to keep him bent half over the bed, her face close to his.

"I know you're going to take Paavo out to Macor in a little while. I just want you to know that even though I won't be there, I'm with you. Okay? I support your decision. I know how hard it will be for you to do this," Chey whispered.

Sander studied her eyes, then swooped in to place a gentle but possessive kiss on her mouth. Straightening after she slipped her fingers from his neck and settled into the pillows, he exhaled a quiet breath and said, "When I think of Mattias and Paavo and Gunner and Natalia, I remember them as kids. Those years when we were into all kinds of mischief, and how protective I was over each and every one. I remember the time Paavo, with his luminous eyes and devilish smile, put twenty crickets in Natalia's favorite pair of riding boots and listened to her scream the walls down. Once, we four boys had a camp out in the woods, bonding over roasted marshmallows, fake sword fights, and a scare in the middle of the night when we thought a bear was right outside the tent. Turned out to be Natalia, getting payback for the crickets. That's what I remember when I think about Paavo facing pre-meditated death. And that's what execution is, when you get down to the bottom line. Killing someone in self defense is different than planning for weeks to administer a lethal injection. Had I come face to face with him in the rubble he made at Ahtissari, I probably would have ended him where he stood. Because it's in the moment, it's life or death *right now*. It wouldn't have been easy, I won't pretend otherwise, but this...this is difficult. I'm still so angry sometimes that I'm surprised *I* didn't push for his death myself. Then the old memories surface and I find it hard to consider ending his life in any way other than a life or death struggle. Those are things I *didn't* admit to in the council meeting, because I wasn't sure the men would understand. And I *do* think death is an easy way out for a man who loathes being imprisoned as much as Paavo. Down deep, I know remanding Paavo to Macor and forcing him to be out of contact with humanity is the worst thing I could possibly do to him." He paused, licked the edge of his teeth. "None of this has been easy. Knowing every single day I wake up that my brother, the one I used to do all those fun things with as children, is probably climbing the walls of an old ruin and slowly going madder than he already is will haunt me for the rest of my days. Losing you and the kids would have changed me as a man, as the person people know as Sander Ahtissari, though, so if this is the way it has to play out, then that's what I'll do."

"I can understand it, even if I don't have siblings. It would almost be the same if I had to do this to Wynn. She might just be a best friend, but we did all those things growing up. We're closer than close, and I love her with all my heart. I can't even imagine having to sentence her to death or lock her away for life. One of the reasons I fell so hard for you was because I loved your compassion and consideration of other people's feelings. If you had gloated and celebrated Paavo's death, I think I would have been disappointed. Just because it's not easy to do what you have to, doesn't mean you won't do what you must. Paavo will get his punishment. I have no doubt of that. The citizens of this country know it, too. Your reputation as a hands-on king, someone whose dedication to his people is legendary, will be what everyone focuses on going forward. Those who can commiserate with your situation will understand." Chey reached out to brush her fingertips along the back of his hand.

Sander smiled down into her face, catching her fingers for a quick, light squeeze. "Thanks. I'm glad I have people in my corner. Mattias, Gunner and Natalia all understand and have publicly backed me. Some members of the council still rail and rant about it, but they'll get over it and be on to the next thing soon."

"That's human nature, I guess. There will always be *someone* who disagrees." Chey smiled when Sander brushed a kiss across her palm, then returned her hand to the covers.

"Exactly. I'd better go get this over with. I want to be back before the storm rolls in." Sander kissed Chey's mouth one more time.

He departed the bedchamber after that, steeling his resolve as he left the castle behind.

* * *

Sander stared down at the ruins of Macor as the helicopter circled overhead. The structure, considered a ruin thanks to the age and state of decay, looked the same as he remembered on his last visit. It wasn't a large fortress, but the stone walls were a foot thick, the front door a heavy slab of iron enforced wood, with windows facing out across both a pasture and woods.

Another chopper carrying Paavo and extra guards followed close behind Sander's craft, aiming for a vacant few acres of flat land suitable to set the birds down.

Sander, with Mattias at his side, disembarked and set out to inspect the changes he had ordered over the last few days. Iron bars covered every window now, giving any occupant a view of the pastures and trees but prohibiting any thought of escape. The front door had been reinforced with more iron as well, along with an extra set of bars tacked to the outside. One of the lower windows had been fitted with a special pass-through slit for delivery of meals on a tray. The bigger problem had been heat.

326

Latvala's winters were brutal and no one would survive within the walls without some kind of system to provide warmth. Fire was out; Sander didn't want to give his brother any kind of weapon to use against guards. So he'd had a separate compartment built for a heater to push warmth in through an iron barred window. The heater itself could not be accessed from within the walls of Macor, thereby reducing Paavo's odds of dismantling the unit for parts that again, might become weapons. Only one room would receive enough warmth to be comfortable—but that was for Paavo to deal with. The single bed had no metal frame, nor wood. It was two double mattresses situated flat on the floor. Sander had ordered the men responsible for Paavo's care to use tranquilizers should Paavo prove difficult on cleaning and pest eradication days. Small cameras situated high in the corners of every room would monitor his brother's actions. The second it appeared Paavo was attempting to escape, the guards would knock Paavo out via the tranquilizers.

Sander had no doubt that Paavo would try every trick in the book to gain his freedom.

Coming around to the front of the fortress, Sander met up with Paavo, who was surrounded by guards. To the lead guard, Sander said, "Everything looks as I asked. Should you or anyone else have questions while on your shift, call Urmas directly."

"What is this, Dare?" Paavo asked, frowning. He wore a simple, neon orange jumpsuit with slip on shoes. The eye-watering color would attract the guard's attention should Paavo make an escape.

"This is where you'll serve out your sentence. I'm sure you remember Macor." Sander met Paavo's gaze. He felt no guilt for what he was about to do.

"You can't be serious," Paavo said with a grating laugh. The whites of his eyes showed, however, and his nostrils flared. "This is no place for a prisoner."

"I've made it all but impossible to escape. Here, you will have no access to other inmates or guards who you might sway with threats of blackmail. You'll be given one hot meal a day and two cold meals, along with enough water to survive." Sander gestured for the iron bars to be opened, and then the heavy door.

Paavo leaned against the guards,

bracing himself from being pushed forward into the fortress. An angry, almost accusing tone accompanied his next words. "This is absurd. It's not insulated beyond the stone and has no heating or light."

"It does have heating, Paavo. I arranged it that way. What it doesn't have is stimulation. No lights, no television, no games, no one else to torture. Here, you will spend the rest of your days and nights contemplating the consequences of your actions." Sander gestured for the guards to escort Paavo inside.

"Wait! Wait--"

The guards did not heed Paavo's protests. Sander followed the group past the door into the main room of the fortress. A large, square base made up the ground floor, with stairs leading to rooms above. There were two doors to other rooms and the barred windows overlooking the terrain beyond the ruin. The main room's ceiling vaulted up two floors, giving a grand sense of space with more high windows allowing light to pour in at angled slants.

"There isn't even a chair to sit in! This is barbaric!" Paavo declared, struggling against the guards. His bound wrists and ankles made it impossible to fight his way free.

"There's a bed in that small chamber over there," Sander said of the shadowy doorway to the right. "That's also the only room that the heater heats fully. The rest fizzles out in this lofty area here and up the stairs."

"You can't do this. You can't--"

"I can, Paavo. I *am*. Now sit on the floor and allow the guards to remove your shackles. Or, if you prefer, we can leave those on, too." Sander would absolutely allow Paavo to live with the restraints for several hours and only remove them after sedation. The guards were all well trained in the use of tranquilizers.

Paavo refused to sit. He snarled at one guard that kneeled to try and get the ankle shackles off.

"All right. Leave them on. Guards." Sander pivoted and exited the fortress. His boots thudded on the stone until he reached the dirt area just beyond the door. The guards filed out behind him.

"Dare! The international community will have a field day with this when they find out. You can't treat a prisoner with this much cruelty!"

Sander ignored Paavo's ranting and

whining. He watched as the guards closed the heavy door, laid the braces in place, and attached no less than three locks through chains that secured the door to an iron plate in the wall. Then, and only then, were the final bars closed over that. Two massive layers to break through, which was beyond any man's means, especially with no tools. There wasn't any other entrance or exit to the building, built that way for security reasons in an age of endless war.

"Dare! *Dare!*" Paavo's voice echoed through the building, barely heard through the thick paned windows.

Sander ignored the faint shouts and faced the guards. They were men chosen specifically for the task. "There are security feeds everywhere. The layers of protection don't stop here. So if he attempts to talk to you for longer than five minutes, troops will be en route here and you'll be questioned. You've already been filled in on what to expect, and what to do—as well as what not to do. Contact Urmas with any concerns."

The guards inclined their heads.

Sander watched the guards retreat to one of the converted outbuildings. There, the men had all the necessities a body required for comfort: heat, water, separate bedrooms for sleeping during shift changes, a small but well appointed kitchen and extra stores of food.

Everything had been taken care of.

Sander looked back to the window, where he could see Paavo pacing the interior of the fortress, already looking for weaknesses and ways out. He heard his name repeatedly, along with threats to his family that hardened his eyes and toyed with his temper.

The last glimpse Sander had of his brother was one he would never forget: Paavo, wild-eyed, panic and realization etched into his features, stalking past the window. Sander turned away then, following his former footsteps back toward the chopper. He heard his name again, fading further and further, until it was just the gentle breeze through the pasture grasses and the whine of the engines as the pilot readied for the flight back to Pallan island.

As he strapped into his seat and placed the headgear over his ears, Sander's mind cast back to happier times in his life. To those scenes he'd described to Chey, when he and his siblings hadn't the stresses and responsibilities they had today. He preferred to recall the affection, the trust, the loyalty the Ahtissari children had once had together rather than the mad man Paavo had become.

This was, he reflected, his final goodbye.

Chapter Twenty-Five

My wife issued me a challenge that I cannot refuse. The challenge is this, right here, my very first (and probably my last) journal entry. I don't feel the need to pour my emotions out on paper like she does, but a challenge is a challenge and, like all the other times, I'll rise to the occasion.

I have no idea what to say. Does that make you happy, Chey? I know you'll read this and laugh. You'll read this with glee and realize that your doting husband can't do journal entries to save his life. Maybe then you won't keep asking me to write things down.

Anyway. What to say. It's peculiar to try and figure what to commit to the page when I'm so cautious about how I project myself in public. Chey would say that this isn't public, it's private, and that's what's so great about it. I can put anything here that I want to and no one but me (and her) will see it.

Even so, even knowing any entries

beyond this initial one are for my eyes only, I feel conspicuous. Talking about the weather (winter has settled in fully now, as we push toward the middle of December) seems humdrum and boring, as does the details of my every day schedule. I know she hopes I'll vent some of my most inner feelings about the bombings and my decision about my brother, but I'm strangely hesitant to pen anything about it. The country is recovering slowly. The citizens were especially horrified that Ahtissari castle was hit with such force, but many have come out to support my decision about my brother's punishment. The council hasn't let me forget, not for one day, that I will be held personally responsible for every single death that occurs should Paavo either escape or somehow convince others to again act in his stead.

Do they not realize I already bear the responsibility of the deaths past? From all three bombings? Because I was not vigilant enough concerning Paavo's imprisonment, innocent people died. The deaths have kept me awake at night and also haunted my dreams. In the time since the incident, I have worked tirelessly to change policies about the security of my borders and our people. The prison has been overhauled, with new systems in place to deal with exactly the kind of situation that led to the last breach.

These actions will not bring the dead back, and I mourn that fact, but it should prevent more in the future. In the aftermath of the destruction, I have forged alliances with both Imatra and Somero. Our cautious meetings have been fruitful, and both Thane and Aleksi have proven to be responsible leaders. Imatra, with Somero and Latvala's help, has begun to recover from Konstantine's reign.

Elias, Emily and Erick have bounced back admirably. None seem to experience fears or worries about the bombing, for which I am grateful. Someone once told me that children are very resilient, and I have seen proof of that here. I adore them more than I can say. Elias is growing more independent and strong willed every day. I have been unobtrusively shaping him into the king he will one day become. Mattias, Gunnar, Leander and several other friends who are sovereigns in their own right have also provided guidance, which I believe will make Elias a well rounded king when the time comes.

Emily is the spitting image of Chey. She

is sweet, kind and has a willful streak a mile wide. She also has me completely wrapped around her little finger. I have given her little 'duties' as princess and she takes them all very seriously.

Erick is currently wading through the waters of the terrible twos. I have to say— he does not seem to be overly afflicted by temper tantrums, but when he throws them, the entire castle is aware he's on a rampage.

Chey is recovering well from the shooting. With the sling gone, one would hardly ever know anything happened with the way she bustles around, doing ten tasks at once. Christmas is almost upon us, so of course she's turned Kallaster into a wonderland of decorations and light. I am thankful every day that she survived both catastrophes and is by my side.

I got more written here than I first thought, so I think I've met and completed Chey's 'journal challenge'. I expect her to gloat for a full twenty-four hours, even if I didn't spill my deepest, darkest feelings onto the page.

Sander, King of Latvala
p.s. I'd better not quit my day job to become a writer.

Sander re-read the entry with a snort. He closed the cover of the leather bound journal and smoothed a hand over the dark surface. There were pages and pages left beyond the one he'd used, pages that, as far as he was concerned, would remain blank. Writing his personal thoughts on paper was not his strong point. He was too private about his inner workings to share them in this particular manner.

Standing from the desk in his personal office, he wandered to the balcony windows of the bedroom suite. Snow fell in fat flakes, creating more layers of white on top of the foot of snowfall that had accumulated during the night. The balcony banister was loaded, though staff members had cleared the balcony itself, as well as the chairs and table, in case Sander and Chey preferred to watch the snow fall outside instead of inside.

He realized he hadn't been disturbed by the kids or Chey in hours and, frowning, crossed the suite and exited into the hall. He checked all the upstairs rooms where the kids usually played— empty. Chey was nowhere to be found. Lifting a hand, he smoothed down the fine hairs at the back of his neck, reassuring himself silently that they were probably all in the kitchen or in the big play room.

The kitchen proved to be empty of his family, as well as the play room. His steps quickened toward the front of the castle, where he spotted Urmas, hands full of folders.

"Have you seen Chey and the kids?" he asked outright.

Urmas halted in place and inclined his head. "Your Majesty. They're right outside." He tilted a look at the double front doors.

"Thanks." Sander didn't bother to remind Urmas that he was free to use his given name in these unofficial surroundings. Pushing outside, Sander caught sight of his children and wife. Chey and the kids were building snowmen in the bailey, not far from the front steps. He smiled at the crooked snowman Elias worked on, and the tiny one Emily constructed with red gloved hands.

The tightness and fear that had begun to constrict his chest eased. If he'd suffered any after effects from the bombings and attacks, it was the extreme unease that settled in when he couldn't easily locate his immediate family. The fear of losing them lingered, occasionally flaring hot and wild.

Trotting down the steps, he waded through the snow drift, already attired in warm winter clothing and waterproof boots. Chey's red sweater, the same red as Emily's gloves, was a beacon that drew him straight to her. She saw him coming and smiled, cheeks flushed from the cold, a wad of snow in her hands.

"Look, Em's building a snow cone!" Chey announced with a laugh, to which Emily stomped a boot with indignation.

"It's a snowprincess!" Emily declared. Her 'snowprincess' was perhaps the size of...a three tiered snow cone.

Sander laughed. "I see that. You've all been busy."

Chey met Sander with a chilly kiss, then proudly eyed her own creation. The snowman was perhaps four feet tall, somewhat cock-eyed from the 'waist' up, with only one twig arm in place. Clearly, she was still working on her masterpiece.

"It looks drunk," Sander said, grinning as he stepped aside before Chey could douse him with snow. He plucked Erick up off the ground. The navy blue coat, beanie hat and tiny gloves all but swallowed the toddler up. Covered in snow dust, Erick laughed and clapped his hands, sending a sprinkle of coldness over Sander's face and throat.

"...well, that backfired," he said with a grunt.

Chey didn't just laugh, she *belly* laughed. Elias bustled busily around his snowman, packing more snow here, there and everywhere. He did pause to grin at his father, but went right back to the project.

Until the first snowball flew through the air.

Sander, smacked in the shoulder with the harmless missile, sent Chey a devious, promising look—except she still had the snow in her hands. And *she* was looking toward another spot in the bailey, where a sudden howl split the air and snowballs rained down.

Mattias, Leander and Gunnar scooped up more snowballs and sent them flying toward the king.

"What are you, five?" Sander shouted when he realized they were under an attack of the snowball kind. Laughing, he set Erick down and encourage his family to send some snowballs right back. "C'mon, Elias, Emily! Get 'em!"

The Great Snowball War was on.

* * *

Chey's favorite part of the Christmas season was the evening after the morning of frantic gift opening, when twinkle lights glowed on a tall tree in a dimly lit room and a fire roared in the fireplace. Decorations had transformed the living area into a festive sanctuary. Ribbon, wreaths, Santas, angels, lights, the huge tree, reindeer, poinsettias—it was all here. The gifts were gone now, the toys hauled off to each child's respective room. Sitting in a cushy chair adjacent to the fireplace, mug of hot cider in hand, Chey relaxed and languished in the ambiance. Although Christmas wasn't a traditional holiday of his country, Sander had embraced the ritual for her. He never complained when she packed the castle with lights and décor, often helping to set it all up because he knew she loved it when he did.

This holiday, Chey had been especially thankful for her family. Several times when the kids had opened their presents, she'd gotten teary-eyed and had been forced to dab the wetness away with tissues. The attack on Ahtissari castle had left lasting scars, even moreso than the shooting, and made her more aware than ever that life was short. She was thankful to have her life and the lives of her children spared when others had not been so lucky.

Sander too had been preoccupied since the attacks. She caught him staring out at the ocean often, or at the snowy landscape of the island, a deeply contemplative look on his face. She knew it had to do with the attacks, with the shooting, and with Paavo. Sander was not a man who made decisions, any decisions, lightly. He also took every loss personally, no matter how many times she or Mattias had put the blame elsewhere. It was just the kind of king Sander was.

Friends from far and wide had pledged any kind of aid Sander needed to help with the recovery, and their presence at Kallaster for days at a time had been a pleasant distraction from the endless task of bringing Latvala back to an even keel.

Drawn from her thoughts by motion near the archway, she glanced from the fireplace to the door. Sander stood there, tilted against the frame, arms crossed over his chest. She smiled. "How long have you been standing there?"

"Long enough. You looked almost too peaceful to disturb."

"You're never a disturbance."

"I'm glad to hear it, because I planned to come in anyway." Which he did, crossing the room to her chair a moment later. He bent to pluck a kiss from her lips.

"It's a good thing, because I totally forgot that there's one more gift to give." She pointed to a gift tucked behind another chair, a one foot by one foot square covered in gold and ivy paper.

"For me?" he asked with a curious look, diverting to the chair to pull the gift from the back.

"Yes." Chey watched Sander take the package to a closer seat. He wore a devilish look all of a sudden.

"This is a boudoir portrait of you, isn't it? That's why I couldn't open it with everyone else here."

Chey laughed. "I hate that you guess all your presents before you open them!"

Sander cackled and eagerly opened the wrapping. A frame appeared, sure enough, with matting creating a square around a little white stick centered in the middle. Not a boudoir painting at all, but a pregnancy test.

A positive pregnancy test.

Chey watched Sander's expression morph from lewd anticipation to excited surprise.

He shot a startled look her way and, with a broad grin, said, "Again?"

Smitten with his excitement at the announcement that their fourth child was on the way, Chey smiled an adoring smile right back at him. "Again."

Chapter Twenty-Six

The weather took a brutal turn in January. Latvala, on pace to surpass all low temperature records, hovered in the single digits at the height of the day, only to sink well below zero when the sun went down. Citizens scrambled to keep warm as the temperature plunged to minus forty, the coldest winter since records began. Power outages occurred, which forced people to use alternate means of heating.

Kallaster relied on fireplaces to help heat the enormous castle, but a chill pervaded the empty rooms and long corridors. Constant shoveling of the bailey took place, so cars could get in and out of the gate.

Chey waited for Sander to finish with an important, urgent meeting, patiently watching the hallway for his presence. Wrapped in a warm wool shawl to keep the chill from her skin, she smoothed a hand over the gentle swell of her belly. It was still too early to tell the gender, but they both wanted to know as soon as possible. He thought it was a girl, she thought it was another boy. As long as the baby was healthy, Chey wouldn't mind either way. It was always fun to wage impossible bets with Sander however, and she secretly adored the way he gloated and preened when he won.

He appeared moments later, looking much more grim than when he'd left her earlier that morning. She noted that he hadn't changed out of the buckskin pants and ribbed pullover of white, much more informal attire than he wore when conducting the king's business with the council.

She straightened and frowned, palm falling away from her stomach. "What is it?"

"Paavo is dead."

"What? How?" Chey touched Sander's arm, searching his eyes for answers. A muscle ticked in his jaw, his body tight with tension.

"The guard house lost power in the blizzard yesterday. The hinterlands took a huge hit, a lot worse than what we had here--"

"It was pretty bad here," Chey said in a

low voice.

"Yes. Anyway, they lost power and couldn't track Paavo's movements in the ruin. Several guards had to dig their way out of their own building, and two got lost in the whiteout, barely able to find the path back to safety. That meant they couldn't reach the ruin until this morning. When Paavo didn't answer their calls, the guards entered the fortress. Although they left plenty of wood inside for Paavo to make a fire in case the power went out, my brother chose to head to the highest floor and sleep in the corner of the tower, where it was coldest. According to the doctors, he died of hypothermia. Out of all the precautions I took so he couldn't hurt himself, I never imagined the weather would be the thing that he used to defy me. In the end, he got his way after all."

Chey listened to the details, privately horrified as the story spun itself out. Paavo was dead by his own choosing. She knew Sander must be running through a gamut of emotions over the ordeal. Her fingers tightened on his arm. "Are you all right?"

He looked past her, fixating on a distant wall. It took him a moment to shape a reply. "I guess I feel guilty, even though I instructed the guards to make sure Paavo had food, water and a way to heat the main room of the fortress—just in case. He's wanted to be gone or exiled for years, and the weather worked to his advantage. I'm trying to tell myself it's better this way, though I suspect it'll take a while for the guilt to go away."

"I'm very sorry it's come to this. Sorry for your guilt, for the conflicting emotions I know you've had since it happened. I know it hasn't been easy." Chey took a step closer, pressing her body lightly against his. She had woken countless nights to find Sander pacing their suite or staring at the ceiling in bed, gaze a million miles away. It wasn't just Paavo in recent weeks but other citizens of Latvala who had succumbed to the bitter cold. The death toll was rising with every new storm that rolled in. Sander had made every provision he could, had gathered teams of volunteers to cut firewood for those in need, those who were at the highest risk if the power went out.

"In a way," he said in a very quiet voice, "I'm glad it's over. Paavo wouldn't have ever recovered and it would have ended me if he'd gotten loose again or managed to use someone to hurt more people. Now we don't have to worry any longer."

"It's still hurtful, I know. Will you bury him in the family plot?" she asked.

He brought his gaze back to her, a glimmer of anger surfacing in his eyes. "No. He doesn't deserve to be buried with any kind of honor. He'll get a spot in the middle of nowhere, even if my mother will have a fit and attempt to sway my decision."

"We haven't heard a peep from Helina over all this," Chey said. "Do you really think she'll come forward with demands?"

"She can talk to the liaisons all she wants. It won't happen. My decision is final and I won't be swayed to interring him in a crypt of his own. I don't intend to be there when they bury him, either, just so you know."

That Sander refused to be there for Paavo's burial told Chey all she needed to know about Sander's state of mind. He might have fought to have Paavo remanded to Macor, thereby sparing Paavo's life, and she knew he often thought back to the time when they were children. But by no means had Sander forgiven Paavo for nearly taking the life of his family, nor the lives of the hundreds lost during the bombing. She suspected there was a lot more anger burning somewhere out of sight, contained only by Sander's strong moral code and his sense of honor.

Woe to Paavo if he had met his brother on the field of battle.

"I know we were supposed to have lunch, but why don't we take the kids to the playroom instead?" Chey had a feeling Sander's appetite had vanished, like her own. Perhaps being around his children would lighten his mood and get him back on even footing. Kids and their innocence had a way of making the darkest days brighter.

* * *

For the next nine weeks, Latvala battled bravely through the frigid winter. Sander, Mattias, Gunnar and Leander joined troops from the military on excursions to the mainland, where they used heavy duty vehicles to deliver food, water and wood to people whose power had been out for days. It was exhausting, tedious work, work that kept Sander's hands and mind busy. He liked nothing more than to be helping the citizens of his country survive the season.

One house in particular, a family of seven with another baby on the way, offered bowls of hot stew to Sander and his crew. Sander shucked his gloves and ate alongside his men, sharing stories with the family of the general state of the country during the weather crisis. Many families had been out of touch with others for days, sometimes weeks, and this particular family was grateful to have as much information as Sander cared to give. Sander ignored the slight tremble of the woman's hands when she refilled his glass or the fleeting stares of her husband. They'd never had royalty in their home before, but he didn't act like royalty; he acted like Sander. He might be the ruler of Latvala, but he was also a person, just like they were.

Sooner than later, boisterous laughter filled the walls of the modest, well kept home, the kids challenging Sander to pretend 'duels' with wooden swords. Those two hours of casual conversation and being with his people healed many parts of Sander that had been damaged since Paavo's attacks. He taught each boy one move to practice and perfect, and informed them that he would be back in the spring to see their progress.

The little girl, with her cherubic smile and blonde curls, shyly asked if she could thread her special ribbon through a braid in his hair. Sander sat in a chair while his men were fit to burst with laughter, and allowed the child to weave her blue ribbon through a skinny braid at his temple. It charmed the girl and, in turn, he was charmed as well.

Suffering the guffaws of his men on the trip home, Sander refused all offers to take the offending ribbon and braid out, preferring to wear it all the way home to show Emily. He felt lighter in the heart than he had in some time.

When he appeared in the master suite doorway, Chey glanced up from paper work spread out on the bed and...stared. She arched one brow, then the other.

Laughing, he nudged the door shut with his boot and shucked his coat, tossing it aside with a negligent flick of his wrist.

"I met the most interesting family today. There was this little girl..."

* * *

About the Author

USA Today Bestselling author Danielle Bourdon was born in Corona, California, but now resides in Texas with her husband and two sons. To date she has penned twenty-four novels and nine short stories. Her interests vary wildly: reading, traveling, photography, graphic art and baking, among others.

There is a black cat named Sheba involved who thinks Danielle's laptop is her personal grooming station.

Check her website for trading card offers, giveaways and announcements!
www.daniellebourdon.com

Follow on Facebook:
www.facebook.com/authordaniellebourdon

More books by Danielle Bourdon:

Romance:

The Latvala Royals Series:

Heir Untamed (Royals Series 1)
King and Kingdom (Royals Series 2)
Heir in Exile (Royals Series 3)
The King Takes A Bride (Royals Series 4)
The Wrath of the King (Royals Series 5)
A Royal Legacy (Royals Series 6)

The Royal Elite Series:

The Royal Elite: Mattias (Book 1)
The Royal Elite: Ahsan (Book 2)
The Royal Elite: Chayton (Book 3)
The Royal Elite: Leander (Book 4)

The Inheritance Series

Escaping Vegas (Book 1)

Jasper and Finley

I'll Say Anything
I'll Do Anything

49942705R00215

Made in the USA
Lexington, KY
26 February 2016